TRUTH:

AN UNANSWERED QUESTION

TRUTH:
AN UNANSWERED QUESTION

Alastair Redfern

2018

Truth: An Unanswered Question - Published by the Rev. Dr. Ashish Amos of the Indian Society for Promoting Christian Knowledge (ISPCK), Post Box 1585, Kashmere Gate, Delhi-110006.

ISBN: 978-81-8465-673-2

Cover Picture: 'He suffered under Pontius Pilate' - from the great East Window of Chesterfield Parish Church (Crooked Spire) by Christopher Webb, 1947, depicting the Apostles' Creed. Reproduced with permission from the Vicar & PCC of Saint Mary & All Saints, Chesterfield.

Laser typeset by

ISPCK, Post Box 1585, 1654, Madarsa Road, Kashmere Gate, Delhi-110006 • *Tel:* 23866323

e-mail: ashish@ispck.org.in • ella@ispck.org.in
website: www.ispck.org.in

All men by nature desire to know.

Aristotle: Metaphysics

Knowledge puffs up, but love builds up.
Anyone who claims to know something
does not yet have the necessary knowledge,
but anyone who loves God is known by him.

St Paul: I Corinthians 8

Contents

Preface

This book tries to make a claim for faith as the basis of human wellbeing, rather than the more utilitarian, empirically measured criteria so widely assumed to be the answer. Behind this marginalisation of faith by our current confidence in human capacities, lies the question of truth. How do we know what is right? And what is knowledge anyway?

As 'postmodernism' seeks to deconstruct the authority of the texts and traditions, and the value placed in them, there is a need to explore not just the truth about 'being', but further, the 'truth' as believing. Much in the Gospel of Jesus Christ is geared towards contributing to this challenge.

The aim is to highlight the opportunity for mission in spaces well beyond the ecclesiastical – presenting mission as a style of journeying and encountering. Church offering resources for a very human procession directed by the mystery of annunciation - through which Good News can be met and absorbed into the everyday unfolding of human life in its shaping for eternity.

Introduction

We live in a time when there is a strong current of self-righteous accusation of 'post-truth' and fake news becoming a dangerous form of manipulation and misleading. The fact that some people seem to manufacture 'truth', or offer hugely biased interpretations of events, drives this alarm. And, of course, it is good that we have an instinct for accuracy, fairness, honesty and transparency. But these undoubted virtues are only part of our approaches to a process of discernment. It is important that such forces shape our perceptions and our values.

Nonetheless this proper and praiseworthy witness to the integrity of public witness and communication too easily hides a very different set of presuppositions – based on an assumption that 'real' truth can be discerned clearly, captured precisely, and communicated directly. This would be the expectation of many who decry the rise of a post-truth society, where personal and limited agendas dictate what is to be noticed, described and shared.

In fact, throughout history, as the art of the historian makes clear, perception, interpretation and presentation has always been selective, and expressive of viewpoints and values located in a particular context or tradition. 'Truth' has always been contested, limited and a contribution to exploring the questions of meaning, identity and purpose.

Which is why, when Pontius Pilate asks Jesus the Messiah "what is truth?" (John 18³⁸) there is no answer: simply silence. In the Gospel of Jesus there is a more profound engagement with the issue of 'truth' – an engagement that can help contemporary evaluations of the post-truth debates, and also highlight the wisdom that Christian apologetic might contribute in an anxious, uncertain and unsure world of claims, counter claims and security-seeking solutions to the issues that human frailties and failings continually produce.

This short book offers an exploration of this urgent contemporary agenda.

ॐ 1 ॐ

What is Truth?

Much of human life is focussed upon trying to discern what is true – of our feelings, our experiences, our relationships, the world around us. Famously, when Pilate asked Jesus, 'what is truth?', our Lord was silent (John 18³⁸).

The question has no simple or complete answer. In this life, like each of us, Jesus was always 'on His way', until the 'third day' (a day of death and a day of new life) when He would 'finish' His work.

Truth is something that unfolds, yet there are ways we can learn to best pursue this completing reality.

Jerusalem can be seen as an important sign of this call and challenge. A holy (whole-making) city for Jews, Christians and Muslims. Even today people look at the city as a site of pressure, question and aspiration. Too many of those who gaze on Jerusalem have completed answers to the question of truth that, for them, the city signifies. But Jesus was more realistic – both about the limitations and struggles of our being on 'the way', and with regard to the key role of signs such as the prophet can highlight. Signs are pointers, not answers.

Soren Kierkegaard, the nineteenth century Danish theologian, challenged the idea that truth is knowledge when he wrote "when it is said, 'thou shalt not contend with God', the meaning of this is that you shall not wish to prove yourself in the right before Him. There is only one way of supporting the claim that you are in the right before God – by learning that you are in the wrong'.[1]

The human desire to be 'right' leads us to put our 'knowledge' in the place of truth. A limited perspective or set of experiences stops deeper engagement with the mysterious unfolding of the 'way'. In fact the key to pursuing 'truth' is to wish to be wrong – to recognise our small place, necessarily depending therefore on the love of God who is always right. Wanting to be right is an assertion of the self, which thus becomes a barrier to receiving love which is more than the self.

Religion is the surrendering of the self, owning that we are always 'wrong'. In an important sense prayer is the desire to own being in the wrong – as individuals, as communities, as nations. Thomas Cranmer captures the essence of this spirituality in the liturgical phrase 'whose service is perfect freedom'. Further, in the Book of Common Prayer confession for Morning Prayer, we acknowledge directly that "there is no health in us". In fact we are 'miserable offenders' – a phrase which can seem to jar in an age obsessed with affirmation by the quickest possible route.

Such giving of the self totally to God, in the way that Jesus calls being a slave (doulos) enables our inevitable wrongness to be taken into His eternal righteousness. Love conquers and embraces all that is less than love in its struggle on the way to this destiny – which we call glory.

We do not control or synthesise 'difference', rather we give ourselves into this different state of being. For Kierkegaard, this 'way' was not progressive, but rather open to moments of "intensification". Thus Jesus, who says, 'I am the Way, the Truth, the Life', offers signs, parables, miracles, meals, discourses – moments of "intensification" that remind us that we are always 'wrong' (in the sense of being so limited) and indicate how better to give this wrongness into the forgiving, receiving love of the Father. In this exchange is the tasting of truth – as a continuing invitation, not a finished answer.

This is why liturgy is so important for nourishing the spiritual life – invitation into a continuing process of atonement through which human wrongness is infused with God's righteousness. There will be a pattern of new beginnings and regular confession of falling short: the rhythm of confession and absolution.

In this sense the way, the truth and the life is a continuing gift from God, so that the repetition of worship becomes a means of receiving new life. Therefore 'truth' can never be captured in generalisations – rather it is always experienced in encounter, as when Pilate stood before Jesus. Truth is not about what we perceive to be 'facts': it is about relationship. Truth will thrive on difference rather than become enmeshed in sameness. Thus truth is an expression of faithfulness, rather than of understanding. Pilate wanted to understand the meaning of truth: Jesus offered a way of sacrificing 'self' into the very different life and agenda of a gracious God.

In this spiritual ecology, Law becomes the art of creating temporary staging posts to identify something about where the journey is leading at a particular time. But this necessary 'law' of politics, religion, culture or personal identify, is always in need of being overshadowed by Grace. Just as science is forever being re-imagined and expressed in new paradigms, so Grace will ever reshape laws and the human systems that provide shelter on the way. This is the profound sense in which Jesus challenges us to recognise the deep reality of having nowhere to lay our head in a definitive sense as we continue on the way. Truth calls us into wholeness, into the Trinitarian refrain 'Holy Holy Holy'[2].

This way does not provide ever greater security or intellectual clarity – but rather an opportunity to intensify the faith that allows love to engage and transform us. God so loved the world.

This is why silence is so important in spirituality. Words very easily become ways of trapping us into our own limitedness. True peace lies beyond understanding. Instead of creating ways of 'knowing' which we use to make a claim on God, we are called to be open to a richer register. The medieval monastic movement would be an example of an attempt to shape human living through the repetition of liturgy as key to giving up the self in order to receive a greater gift.

In this way the flux of change which characterises 'the way' can be placed into the constancy of God's faithfulness. Then 'truth' becomes the art of trusting response and continuing reflection – recognising that each of us is part of an unfolding, amazing, gracious project which Jesus calls the Kingdom.

Hannah Arendt, following Augustine, calls this instinct to respond to the journeying 'natality'[3] : an energy to be creative in ourselves, always in relation to others. Such natality or giving birth to new life, can never be reduced to producing 'selfies'. It is a force for a common good, which therefore requires institutions to provide focus and effectiveness. The temptation of institutions is to solidify such systems into 'rightness': knowledge expressing truth. The key challenge for an institution in the spiritual ecology of the Kingdom is to provoke a continuing ownership of being wrong – by the structures and by the participants, so that new life and wisdom can be received. Participation in owning our 'wrongness' is the foundation of prayer that seeks, more than confirmation of what it thinks it already knows, and opens up those praying to receiving a love that empowers and initiates action on the way.

Thus institutions and individuals can be continually renewed – a process of incarnation – the Spirit of truth ever becoming embodied in human fleshliness and materiality. The way will be always unpredictable as new opportunities and openings arise, thus a journey of faith rather than knowledge.

Identity is always being unveiled and revealed. The climax of the New Testament is a Book of Revelation.

Yet the proclamation of the Christian Gospel, by John the Baptist and by Jesus, begins with the word 'Repent' – to turn round and take self from the centre. This is the foundation of daily confession in our prayers. Thus, to be baptised is to be bound in to a body. To be born is to become part of a family, a community. In these intimate but universalizing contexts the 'wrongness' of our limited human perspective can be drawn into a greater righteousness, through being made right with others as part of the Kingdom project. The path is that of participation in a particular kind of truth, unfolding through a 'way' shaped by a particular 'Life'. This is why prayer is often offered through Jesus Christ, our Lord.

Such love offers ordering through privileged institutions. Marriage, the family, the 'city' as local community, the nation, the universal family of God's people – each place of ordering is one of continuing natality always along a certain way, through which the wrong can be made righteous.

These substantial 'shapers' of human living are a vital guard against the empty freedoms of contemporary liberalism, which simply privileges the self, while allowing those paradigmatic 'institutions' of modern society such as Amazon, Google or Facebook, to claim ever absolute powers in the trading of knowledge as truth, and answers as an adequate outcome to human needs. What is so often lacking is a humble sense of the penultimacy of enterprise and the 'wrongness' of any particular answer or outcome.

Nietzsche termed this tendency the emergence of a 'will to power' in human kind, which heralded the 'death of God'. Creatures becoming the Creator with religious rituals relegated to a small place in the tapestry of public and private life. The measure of human life becomes power and possession: not wrongness with nowhere to lay the head. The excess of grace as love is replaced by a scramble for an excess of measurable 'power' around the self and, inevitably, over against others. Thus 'Truth' is not located in an emerging common good gifted by Love, but is focussed, measured and expressed in finalizing outcomes and immediately experienced satisfactions.

Jacques Derrida characterises people of genuine religious faith as 'those who think that they do not have the right to judge, that a priori they forgive God for whatever God does"[4]. Such humility and dependence seems to be increasingly out of place in a world seeking firmer signs of security and wellbeing. The same was true of Pilate and all that he requested. 'What is Truth?' was a question demanding a clear and implementable 'answer'. Jesus remained silent, and then was carried on His Way, a Life proceeding into the Truth, through the crucifixion of the flesh.

Discernment of truth is a spiritual rather than a scientific process – a journey but never a result. The resources are not just the materialness and immediacy of human experience, but always the deeper currents within these arenas of existence. Hiddenness is a key characteristic of truth, and its manifestation is enabled through humility (we are always wrong) and hope (we are glad to receive more). Humility and hope are the engines of prayer, owning woundedness and opening us up to the spirit of wholeness: the Holy Spirit.

This is why the voiceless and the marginalised have such an important contribution to make to the spiritual journey and the identity of the church. Participation in this Holy Spirit becoming manifest is by way of becoming one with the Christ who died for us all, so that new life can grow. Entering into the mystery of atonement always precedes and shapes the forming of idealism. Owning the wrong is key to enabling the right, the un-covering of "a power which can lift us above our sins into a life perennially made new".[5] Such life is essentially a dependent life which we cannot source ourselves. In more technical language St Paul talks about the mystery that only 'by grace we are saved through faith' (Romans 5[2]).

Thus, according to Egerton, in owning our wrongness, our continually missing the truth, 'we are lifted above sin by a new energy which we receive, but do not create,"[6] and this new birth is therefore, not a change we achieve, but a change that we experience, wrought in us by a power that we know to be not our own. This new life is sustained not by the self, but by participation in the sharing of love, focussed and expressed through a relationship with a Person who is truth. Key indicators of the presence of this Person in this earthly context are the lives of those most obviously dependent and crying out for healing grace – the hungry, the thirsty, the stranger, the naked, the sick, the prisoner (Matthew 25[31-46]).

Endnotes

[1] Claire Carlisle, Kierkegaard's Philosophy of Becoming: State University of New York 2005, p64.

[2] Alastair Redfern, Living in the Trinity, ISPCK 2018.

[3] Pamela Sue Anderson, New Topics in Feminist Philosophy, Springer 2010, p14.

[4] J. D.Caputo, M Dooley, M J Scanlan: Questioning God. Ideiol U. P. 2001 p83.

[5] H. Egerton, Liberal Theology and the Ground of Faith, Pitman 1908, p98.

[6] Ibid, p94.

✄ 2 ✄

Inner Illuminations

Carl Schmitt, a German philosopher in the twentieth century, characterised the liberal agenda emerging from the strengthening systems of nineteenth century socialisms and solidarity, as being a process for endless debate. There was an irony, a paradox in the parallel growth of confidence in truth as scientifically 'proved' knowledge, and the emerging fact that increasing individual freedom gives rise to complex stresses about identity, values and viewpoints. As 'context' became ever more refined and particular, so pluralism created a huge challenge to inclusive ways of understanding and acting. There was more openness to the exploring of a journey on the 'way', yet the tools were too easily assumed to be the scientific ones of psychology, sociology and other 'human' sciences.

The Christian gospel takes seriously the importance of testimony, for individuals and for communities, and owns the important role of 'law' in judging within a common and conjoining framework. Jesus announces the gift of an Advocate – the Holy Spirit, and uses the positive term 'commandments' (John 14$^{15\text{-}16}$). But the Sermon on the Mount (Matthew 5) reveals that these frameworks need to be inhabited by a spirit of generous self-giving to others, and continuing acknowledgement of God's deeper purposes.

The model proposed in the Gospel is that of the Kingdom – a frame for citizens to share a common good. Key resources are specific reference points that indicate a deeper agenda and perspective:

- go show yourself to the Priest

- attend the synagogue and the Temple

- Pilate would have no role unless it was given to him from above, both by the Emperor and by God

- Parables begin: 'a certain king'

This monarchical framework presupposes a certain kind of loyalty and discipline. Testimony framed and evaluated through representation, particular vocations and an agreed set of laws. One of the problems for Church leadership and decision making in our consultative and democratic age is that those who have not been trained or 'licensed' to operate within the agreed doctrinal framework, tend to make contributions which assume a priority being given to personal experience, at the expense of owning laws which discipline the personal in order to enable the communal.

Much oversight of the church as a public, representative body, is tempted to settle for a permissive pluralism that in fact, simply fuels incoherence and a gospel which undermines rather than fulfils the covenant which the church is invited to inhabit. Thus agendas focus upon promoting personal viewpoints seeking 'rights' through contractual style agreements, rather than owning a common discipline to prioritise the 'frame' the church has received. Truth too easily becomes an attempt to make the church and Christian discipleship in our own image.

However, the essence of Anglicanism is the dynamic of conflicting testimonies 'or Fundamentalisms in dialogue'[1], but always within a discipline of the law that provides the staging post in receiving grace. This is a crucial grace which guards us against discipleship being expressed through rhetoric, rather than the humble sense of wrongness that enables openness to divinely gifted reference points.

Christ is our king and offers a way into a discernment which can accept shaping as the path towards freedom. Hence the key role of institutional forms and 'legal' codes. And yet, even as we observe such divinely given markers, we remain servants of a discernment which will inevitably produce the seeds of its own destruction, to enable further re-formation.

Thus there need to be signs for public illumination. Our temptation is to craft such signs into systems which work by narrowing understanding into rules and procedures. Rather, illumination arises from the questioning and challenge that can raise horizons and help to see new possibilities. Theodore Adorno termed this process one of creating 'constellations' that give expression to what we can receive by being open to these further possibilities.[2] Seeing new things is rarely a mind-blowing revelation of something from totally outside of our experience. Even St Paul's illumination on the road to Damascus was earthed through immediate blindness and the necessity of engaging directly with his 'enemies' (Acts 9).

The new 'constellation' that undergirded Paul's whole approach to being a minister of a Gospel bringing public illumination to Gentiles and Jews alike, was to keep hold of current perceptions, such as the Law, the Temple, the spirituality of dependence deep in an exiled, wandering people, while finding ways of increasing the range and possibilities of further connections. Through this process the digging deeper into current resources, and into the intimations of grace emerging from ownership of human 'wrongness', combined to open up further vistas for guidance and future aspiration. In this way the recognition of constellations can become redemptive, not merely affirmative. Illuminations for journeying rather than for settlement or idolising of the status quo. This redemptive spirit encourages, chastens and opens up the vista of utopia – the Kingdom which is 'no place' except a destination in glory.

And, of course, such glimpsing of new constellations, involves not just the vital process of noticing new life and possibilities, it also involves moving away from previously cherished or constraining vistas. Homelessness is the continuing cost of spiritual discernment within this Gospel framework. As the Gospels make clear, much illumination occurs on the margins of established systems, relationships and values.

For this reason immediate appearances have to be owned as always transitional, open to being negated or neglected: 'truth' always contains the untruth of a merely present perspective. Adorno becomes more specific by showing that identity thinking therefore can cause violence by forming classificatory judgements which only work by suppressing possibilities.[3] In this way the continuously creative power of love becomes blocked. Our Western tendency to focus upon identity can create a false and damaging understanding of 'truth' which becomes reduced to the criterion of immediate personal pleasure. This creates a closure to the unsettlement of future unknown possibilities – a denial of the vital role of potential being called into new forms of living.

This damaging delusion can be countered by prayer: 'the purposeful giving of attention to the particularity of phenomenon in the world'[4] so that illumination can be given. Christian spirituality acknowledges the sign and model of Jesus as an indicator and originator of this power and process of prayer. The way of revelation which un-covers new life amidst the realities of present experience. A key danger to this possibility of prayer is our increasing dependence upon the overwhelming forces of administration, designed to capture and preserve identities. The problem of law disconnected from grace.

Public identities need this fluidity, and the courage to be broken open into new constellations, as much as private lives. Gillian Rose showed how systems of thinking have come to dominate the possibilities of illumination: she points to the will to power (Nietzsche); Being (Hiedegger); the virtual

(Deleuze); différance (Derrida) and power (Foucault) as key examples. Each can become a limiting scheme of public illumination, calling for 'deepening' within a particular set of perspectives.[5] The revolutionary power of incarnation as the divine indwelling of the ordinariness of human living becomes circumscribed by the limits of a particular moment of the human imagination – however inspired or resonant that offering might be.

Rose recognises the importance of law – as being based upon 'representations' that always require interpretation and judgement, while being open to the contribution of further evidence. The liturgy could be seen as a living courtroom for such continuing adjudication. There is a dynamic mix of testimony, confession, absolution, remembering resources already given and cherished, testing perceptions and seeking further illumination in prayer, and accepting moments of judgment and peace. There is an important role for representative, overseeing figures and a ritual to ensure key resources and roles are enabled to contribute too. The outcome is a sense of 'blessing' – a contentment to be in that light of that moment, yet a recognition that the process, with all its risks and challenges, will always need to be repeated.

Good practice safeguards against the undue magnification of particular perspectives, and holds the ring for the inevitable complexities of a truly catholic connectivity which will need to be always emerging. In this sense any genuinely common life will be shared through a mystery which 'opens the gate to a thousand fresh enquiries'.[6]

Each enquiry can become an excluding, totalising 'empire' of control and constraint, or a gift with the emergence of a richer public illumination. This reality is the litmus test for different schools of theology and styles of churchmanship. Gifts can contribute to what Figgis would celebrate as 'a way of adventure', requiring the asceticism which owns what one has been given and yet schools it to be focussed in the service of God's greater agenda. He writes, 'The supreme difference of the Christian religion is this fact, that it is the gift of a new life, not a code, or a creed, or an achievement, but a spirit given'.[7] This gift is to 'a creature dying': the reality of always being wrong. Thus the gift is not just revelatory, but also redemptive. This is the richer register we can discover in looking deeper.

Atonement in Jesus Christ is the definitive expression of this life-giving movement, issuing from freely accepted sacrifice. The action which gives life to the dead as an expression of love. Inviting participation in a transforming reality, which does not simply translate love into welfare as system, but rather creates a shared intimacy, always opening into greater depth.

This 'route' for the way is therefore always one of disturbance, through the continuing recognition of being wrong, and of dialectic with other illuminative resources. Yet the essential gift comes from within. Jesus is clear that "the Kingdom is within you". Paul calls this the experience of living 'in Christ', being indwelt by the power of the Holy Spirit. Intellectual endeavour and social organisation will be always subsequent and temporary expressions of this inner experience. This kind of truth is a great leveller, because it works by breaking down in order to enable appropriate building up. Thus the first shall become last and the last first. And this is always a way of indirect communication: glimpses of glory and struggles to own temptations to being right.

This provokes a challenge to the too easy presumption of neutral, objective knowledge. This kind of 'control' will inevitably be achieved only through the administration of 'violence' to a deeper possibility.[8] The ultimate expression of this tendency in the twentieth century would be the holocaust.

Given the tendencies towards the colonisation of meaning and purpose recognised by Gillian Rose, we may need to have a new campaign against the processes of 'enclosure'. Just as medieval Europe found strength and identity through the enclosure of common lands to promote greater efficiencies, thus circumscribing the lives of all but those who wielded the powers of enclosure – so our own century may need to consider a similar dilemma. The power focussed by such 'enclosing' systems as Google and Facebook creates 'controls' as significant as those of intellectual ideologies. In response, individuals are surviving by retreat into private "enclosure". Public life and public illumination is fracturing – not to let in more light, but to be marginalised by the private powers of enclosure, created by huge corporations and gladly mirrored by individuals seeking spaces of personal safety and security.

Each of us, in relationships as in communities, needs the opportunity to discover new constellations which cross the current boundaries of control – public and private. The history of the church shows that prayer can be the key to this subversive power – schooling humility that opens up to the possibilities of richer wholeness or holiness.

Such a spiritual approach provides 'power' to relate creatively to the deeper complexities of life, which cannot be easily captured by systems or by reason. Examples would be family, marriage, illness, career, ageing, natural disasters, economic hardships, marginalisation... Such essential elements of living cannot be boundaried in a narrow way, but require a measure of trust (faith) in powers, persons, roles and rituals that can cherish, re-member (i.e. re-make) and redirect. The utilitarian tendency which seems to be becoming the 'common' ground on which we can all stand, whatever our 'differences' is a barren place of concealed violence and power imbalance. Only a deeper engagement with self and with society will open up more proven and more effective resources for flourishing through the inevitable unevenness of the human journey.

Our way needs this truth and life, present but needing deeper discernment than our hurried approach seems to allow.

Endnotes

[1] Alastair Redfern, Being Anglican, DLT 2000, p9.

[2] P. Hayes, Immanent Transcendence, Continuum 2012, p 35. See also M. Foucault, The Archaeology of Knowledge, Tavistock 1972.

[3] P. Hayes, Immanent Transcendence, Continuum 2012, p138.

[4] Ibid., p139.

[5] W. Lloyd, Law and Transcendence, Palgrave 2009, p4.

[6] J.N. Figgis, The Fellowship of the Mystery, Longmans 1914, p3.

[7] Ibid., p19.

[8] M. Foucault. Madness and Civilisation, Tavistock 1971.

ॐ 3 ॐ

Giving and Receiving:

Sacrifice with Secrecy

Much of our sense of reality, and of trying to negotiate the challenges life brings, is determined by a strong economic sense of values. We live as producers and consumers – of goods, of relationships, of communities and societies. This terrain can be negotiated selfishly, for my own benefit and interests, or sacrificially, for the wellbeing of others. Yet the model of economic transactions persists. There seems to be an inevitable dynamic of give and get.

Spirituality and the various religious frames that nourish and hold it has often operated along similar lives. Many religions focus upon the centrality of sacrifice. Power, materially and spiritually, is thought to be forces needing control and development. Therefore rituals and theologies of sacrifice are used to make offering to God/the Gods as the first stage in an economic transaction that will deliver a reciprocal response. Giving creates obligation – not just between human parties, but between the human and the divine.

Thus much spirituality is grounded in a set of economic transactions based upon the inevitability of a dynamic between giving and receiving. A dynamic that involves creatures and Creator.

The counter cultural phenomenon of the atonement wrought in Jesus Christ is that the One to whom debt is owed, before who there needs to be recognition of being in the wrong, or incomplete – is simultaneously the creditor who has provided this life. The One who gives life is the One who restores that life from the wrongness we tend to choose. Gift is followed by gift – not a demand for something in return. Christ takes our sins upon himself – in Pauline terms.

This double gifting can be seen to be creating an even more pressing obligation on the debtor given such transforming credit. But, in fact, the Giver and the Gift are expressions of a consistent, continuing outflowing of love, from the Father (Giver), through the Son (Gift) in the power of the Holy Spirit (continuing gift of credit and grace).

Those receiving the gift are to respond first not with a 'balancing' return gift – but with thanks and praise. The response is to receive with thanks. The sacrifice of Christ is embraced in Eucharist – a public thanksgiving for Giver, Gift, Continuing Gift. In this context, there will be a stronger sense of being in the wrong, of confession, of desire – but true desire is not human emotion to pay back what might be due. Rather it is the humility to become a conduit and a bearer of that freely given and restoring love so that others may taste it too. The gift is given in order to be handed on – a commission to be an agent of the giving of generous love.

Sacrifice for Christian discipleship is receiving this triple gift of Father, Son, and Holy Spirit, so that new life can transform the recipient into a participant in the outflow of the saving love of God. The context can never be reduced to a 'personal' or 'group' transaction between recipient and Donor. Yet this too easily becomes the position and 'identity' of Christian people. The economic transaction is manifestly the way of the world. Life lived through its materiality: reduced to capturing and controlling immediate experience and calculable possibilities. How much of our spiritual lives is pursued within this market economy of rewards and punishments: just desserts?

Sacrifice in Christ is a making space for the indwelling love of God, which puts every economic transaction into a different perspective: Participation in the life of the Trinity[1]. Thus all experiences of gift and of goodness become the leaven of a very different set of values and processes. The difference between giving and participation is crucial. Unless discipleship allows us to shift from the former to the latter, we will remain trapped in a worldly economy of measurable change – and shape our spiritualties accordingly. To receive love is to become caught up in love, and part of love's outflow to those needing such transforming grace. This is a love that renounces self and risks journeying on the way of ever new constellations and possibilities. Sacrifice begets sacrifice. A key element of this generous ecology of love is secrecy: guarding against knowing. As in Matthew 3 where Jesus advises on the working of the triple gift through the outflowing of love:

> "when you give alms, do not let your left hand know what your right hand is doing; so that your alms may be done in secret, and your Father who sees in secret will reward you".

There is a knowing which can only be the property of the Father. Our perspective is the humility of knowing 'that we are always wrong' and the hesitancy therefore in claiming any righteousness for ourselves or our actions. Thus even our witness can only be 'traded' by God – not directly by ourselves. This 'truth' raises important questions and challenge for the whole tradition of Sacrificial Christian service to others. Under pressure we are to trust that God will give us words to say.

This perspective is reinforced in verse 6 of the same chapter in Matthew:

> "But whenever you pray, go into your room, and shut the door and pray to your Father who is in secret, and your Father who sees in secret will receive you."

Secrecy undermines the whole rationale and manifestation of the economic, which depends upon seeing and measuring what you seek to get. Further, disciples are enjoined not just to act in secret, but to cultivate secrecy as key to this alternative, non-economic ecology through which the public illumination of the coming kingdom can be made manifest and gradually unfolded. Hence in Matthew 6[17]:

"But when you fast, put oil on your head and wash your face, so that your fasting may not be seen by others, but by your Father who is in secret, and your Father who sees in secret will reward you."

The triple gift works through a secrecy that creates a new ecology of faith – in what can be sensed, tasted, but not fully seen or known. Thus the key tools are not strategies to produce measurable transactions, but rather, the self-denying disciplines of alms, prayer and fasting. Too often these elements are seen by Christians and others as part of the permissible outworkings of the faith, rather than being recognised and used as the key levers. As a result the practice of private prayer and public worship become places of 'economic' transactions, producing great devotion but not fully releasing the triple gifts of love. The place of alms, prayer and fasting need to be central markers of the authenticity of private devotion and public worship.

Such sacrifice into secrecy is a continuing step into the unknown – an ever renewed step of faith. The 'rewards' will never be measurable, but always focussed through a sense of participation in grace offered for the salvation of the world. In our contemporary climate such a perspective needs to play a more prominent part in the necessary formulation of policy and strategies. There must always be space for encounter beyond what is known or anticipated, so that new seeds can grow in secret and surprising fruits be discovered. Much of the teaching of the Gospels explores this kind of organic imagery. St Paul grasps a similar insight when he challenges the Philippians to 'work out your own salvation in fear and trembling', Philippians 2^{12}. He continues 'For it is God who is at work in you, enabling you both to will and to work for his good pleasure' (Philippians 2^{13}).

The key to 'seeing' within such secrecy is light which stirs from within – a deeper illumination than the shapes and shadows of the material, tradeable world. Also in Matthew 6^{22-23} Jesus confirms that:

> "the eye is the lamp of the body. So if your eye is healthy your whole body will be full of light, but if your eye is unhealthy, your whole body will be full of darkness. If then the light in you is darkness, how great will be the darkness."

Seeing depends upon the illumination from within. The light that lightens every creature (John 1^{1-14}). Christian spirituality and worship is an attempt to own the complexities of 'natural' light in the world we inhabit, and to seek a different source of illumination from within. The mystery of the secret seeing of the Father which issues in the reward of the triple gift of love: a gift which commands a generous, self-sacrificing response.

In this sense Christians recognise that sacrifice enables blessing, which issues into thanksgiving. And such an approach to sacrifice means that death is no longer the ending of a particular life, but an opening into the fuller participation to which the triple gift of love calls us. Death becomes not an end, but, as for Jesus in the process of Holy Week and Easter, a gateway which marks the completion of sacrifice into the secret of salvation, and the fuller transformation of the potential we have been tasting and pursuing. Sacrifice becomes the summation of the gifting and the fulfilment of the secret. In the works of St Augustine – you 'receive what you are'.[2]

In this life sacrifice is the way of making space for the recovery of the triple gift of love. It operates not by measurable transactions – the economic – but more secretly, more mysteriously, through signs, irruptions, silences, echoes. Luther puts it very succinctly: 'we do not offer Christ as a sacrifice ... but Christ offers us ... we offer ourselves as a sacrifice along with Christ'.[3] Thus, at the end of the Eucharist, the measurable manifestation of 'community' is dissolved into more secret and unmeasurable mission and ministry: 'Go in peace to love and serve the Lord'.

The temptation to prioritize institutions, knowing and systems, is dissolved into the uneven complexities of the wider world.

As Colossians states, 'He disarmed the principalities and powers and made a public example of them, triumphing over them in Him' (Colossians 2^{8-10}).

Yet in our potential confusion and insecurity, we can be assured that 'when we do not know how to pray as we ought ... that very Spirit intercedes with sighs too deep for words' (Romans 8^{26}). As a result of this Divine giving and our receiving, encountered within the secrecy of the inner life, light and love are enabled to flow anew through the disciple as sign, encouragement, and unfolding fulfilment – amidst all the apparently measurable realities of our challenges and ordered responses. A deeper flow of grace acts as salt and leaven: agency of transformation and a development sustainable into eternity.

Endnotes

[1] Alastair Redfern – Living in The Trinity, ISPCK 2018.

[2] Ed. J.E. Rotelle, The Works of St Augustine, Vol. 7, Sermon 272, New City Press 1993.

[3] Ed. E.T. Bachmann, Luther's Works, Vol 35, A Treatise on The New Testament, Fortress Press 1960.

ॐ 4 ॐ

True Justice:

The Power of Love

The interconnectivity of human living, with the call to create systems for security and welfare, and the danger of enclosing such wisdom in a way which can hamper the light of love which Christ raises up within – this testing and amazing agenda is especially played out around issues of justice, including those relating to gender.

Love is always embodied as we navigate the way, the truth and the life. There needs to be relationship and degrees of cooperation. Moreover bodies are sites of desire and of vulnerability – open both to the moment and to an agenda from beyond.

We live in an age of increasing loneliness and isolation – individuality exposed as lacking. We need to recover a confidence in institutions, called by God for the better fulfilment of His purposes (Romans 13). B.F. Westcott put the matter succinctly, "it was fashionable to regard a state as an aggregation of individuals bound together by considerations of interest or pleasure ... whereas ... the family and not the individual is the unit of human life .... and the family, nation, the race ... cannot be broken up by any effort of the individual will.[1]

Human being is a social condition, framed by essential and foundational structural arrangements such as family, community, society, church. Intimacy needs to be institutionalised, as the ground of placing self creatively in the wider contexts through which purpose and meaning can be better discerned and pursued. Virtue was a word used by Westcott's generation in the nineteenth century to describe the signs of that private and public illumination through which the gift of love might be received, shared and grown. These structures for self-sacrificing love to be tested and expressed are to be vehicles of an ever greater inclusivity knit into the receipt and the sharing of love.

Moreover such 'visible' shapers of our spiritual maturing need to be regarded with the wisdom that discerns temptations towards creating controlling enclosures, and thus inhabited with the wisdom of accepting the place of secrecy and the possibility of as yet unknown development. There needs to be a living authority in such arrangements, and the commitments to sacrificial giving which they enable, so that there is neither a static conformity, nor easy compromise to enforce the outcome uncritically.

This is why the way of such 'institutional' life needs to unfold not through neat organisations but through 'a way of suffering and tears', refusing to tread the path of easy partisanship.[2] Organic growth maintains certain structuring that is consistent with the offering of the birthing of life and its being enabled into further development.

Virtue will always be surrounded by ambiguity, but a key driver will be the inclusive power of love pushing back against the excluding love of power. This agenda is approached, according to Jean Luc Nancy, by 'the sharing of voice'.[3]

The unfinishedness of human living requires both holding and changing into newness. But the method should not be based on the seemingly simple mechanism of trading resources and rights.

This is illustrated by the proper concerns of feminism, which, as Simone de Beauvoir recognised, should not simply mimic the route hitherto taken by men, creating a 'feminine domain'. Beneath the hugely generalised nature of this understandable push back against gender-based discrimination, there is a deeper challenge to include more voices, since 'the fact is that every concrete human being is always singularity situated'. (Simone de Beauvoir).[4] The way to ensure greater progression towards more shared voices is to link the institutional shifts about rights and rules based on gender, to the forces 'of friendship and generosity' which better carry the secret but effective powers of love. There needs to be space and opportunity for the newness offered by the gift of love to enable the struggle to amend and yet honour what has so far been granted. Equality easily becomes a mono-sound demanding conformity from voices living with more subtle pressures and opportunities. Differences are not to be eliminated, but handled more creatively, within the primal shapers Westcott discerned in human history.

This embracing of more voices will involve the invention of new ways of organising and holding relationships, always willing to be more open to transformation, rather than seeking to solidify current experiences as finished totalities. For commentators, like Luce Irigaray, the role of citizenship becomes a key resource, putting personal and communal relations within the political arena presupposed by a kingdom.

Citizenship links each person with the reality of representation and the inhabiting of space. Traditionally woman has provided a 'place' for man, as a companion, home-maker and child-rearer. She is his original home (the womb) and 'she continues to house him, when he needs housing, outside of his world in civic life".[5] This has meant that woman, as a place for someone else, has had no place of her own: but has always been defined as a mother or daughter. The issue then becomes how women can be 'present' as themselves, and also be represented in the public sphere.

For Irigaray the answer lies in a revaluing of 'the couple'[6] – as a primary formative place for receiving, returning and sharing love. Such an insight sits uncomfortably with contemporary emphases upon the individual and the accompanying recognition of the plurality of possible relationships – not just heterosexual.

The task for Christian discernment is to value love received sacrificially (the signs being alms, prayer and asceticism or fasting – all means of modelling the self as second) and to celebrate the new things such grace can bring. This movement will certainly bring new and different life to traditional institutions such as marriage and the family. Nonetheless there remains a powerful temptation for experiences of love to be assessed through the more personal lens of the self, and then manifested in new 'enclosures' which seek to capture these moments – whereas they too are part of a greater unfolding drama of salvation. The direction will, of course, proceed by way of secrecy, rather than through militantly claimed rights and models. Love works through intimacy first, institutions subsequently.

In the lively debate about marriage there needs to be a careful commitment to 'Christian marriage' as a privileged place for the kind of sacrifice which allows the triple gift of love to be received and then expressed – for others. The outcomes will always be political, never merely for private satisfaction.

The image of God is manifest in the creation of male and female – a coupling which becomes a touchstone for human fulfilment, and yet an indication of the possibilities of dissolution into the self and the idolisation of 'knowledge'. This tension between fulfilment through contributing to creation, being in the image of the Creator, and the many ways in which there can be deviations and repudiations of such possibilities, forms the stuff of religious and political endeavours. The aspiration for completion through fulfilment and the apparent reality of a state which 'falls' well below this kind of paradise, by the privileging of desire and knowing simply in terms of human experience and constructions.

Justice becomes the art of discerning the dynamics between the ideal of fulfilment and the challenge of fallenness. In the story of Adam and Eve in Genesis this issue of justice is played out most particularly through the fact of gender. The potential for owning the reality of being 'wrong' and thus open to the healing, restorative power of the triple gift of love is continuously undermined by temptations to miss this mark (ie. sin) and focus on other more immediate agendas – which in the story of Adam and Eve, are symbolised by giving priority to knowledge, at the expense of humility and the secrecy which does not allow 'knowing'.

The sacrament of marriage, and the promise of commitment through the gift of grace to continue through 'better or worse, sickness and health, wealth or poverty'[7] – was the way in which the church tried to institutionalise the sacrifice towards the other which God's love could inhabit and embrace. Righteousness thus could be given to enable sacrifice to grow.

The development of appreciation, and even devotion to the Virgin Mary provided a complementary model of justice: righteousness given to the individual to be expressed by a commitment to celibacy. Such a consecrated state was seen to be a way of playing a proper part in the right ordering of society and its communities. It was never considered to be simply a mark of individual identity. Such consecration provided an important basis for friendship, and thus for a more public persona.

Through this prism of gender and sexuality there was an attempt to explore institutional arrangements to enable the 'justice' of right relationships, as a blessing to the callings of individuals, and as a proper container for the harnessing and sharing of love and affection more widely.

One of the complexities of the twenty first century debate about justice, gender and sexuality is the temptation to expand the existing institutional arrangements of marriage in order to include many more shades of sexual preference and permutations of relations (hence the LGTBI++ phenomenon). Or, there is a movement to abolish such 'constraints' in favour of a more openly free market approach to sexual identities and relationships, based upon the presupposition of individual autonomy and rights – with all the resulting chaos in terms of the stabilities needed for justice to be both recognised and maintained.

As the complexities of sexual awareness and means of fulfilling relationships with various degrees of commitment – from practical to ontological – are expanding, justice may require a more careful search for the new life that the triple gift of love can bring, including an important assessment of the foundational status of gender difference in terms of institutional arrangements and models. The fact that revelation is so often the outcome of being willing to accept the importance (and humility) of 'secrecy' should provide an important message to debates so often dominated by shrill voices proclaiming the 'truth' as known through individual experience. This part of the journey of Justice, and the continuing contribution of gender, needs to become much more central to the Christian exploration of our vocation to new life – not least in terms of the urgent need for righteousness to be recognised as enclosing the structures of family, community and society, rather than simply being a confirmation of individual inclinations.

The developing appreciation of Justice will be key to enabling a proper handling of gender and sexuality issues being quite properly raised. Within such an exploration, the understandable interest in framing sexual desire must not be pursued without an equally urgent emphasis upon how justice can be properly served by friendship as a site for fulfilment and wholeness (holiness). At the root of human intimacy lies the twin instincts for the commitment called 'marriage' and the structuring of varying degrees of empathy and affection that we call friendship. The two offer an important range of possibilities for making love a public witness and contribution.

Endnotes

[1] S. Morgan, Faith, Sex and Purity: the religio-feminist theory of Ellice Hopkins, Women's History Review 200, Vol. 9, p20.

[2] A.E.J. Rawlinson, Theology and Church of England, SPCK 1958, p19.

[3] Ed L. Lansclof and S.H. Watson, Reinterpreting the Political, SUNY, 1998, p8.

[4] Ed L. Lansclof and S.H. Watson, Reinterpreting the Political, SUNY, 1998, p79.

[5] Ed. E.A. Holmes and L.Skol, Breathing With Luce Irigaray, Bloomsberg 2013, p20.

[6] Ibid.

[7] Book of Common Prayer, The Form of Solemnization of Matrimony.

❦ 5 ❧

The Seeds of Truth:

The Mystical Task

Each person is born into a set of twin possibilities. On the one hand, birth creates a private, unique individual. And yet that unique life can only have meaning and potential as part of a more public, plural reality. Thus there are two seemingly different ways for the seed of life to grow – as a person, and as part of a public realm.

For much of human history, the personal has been clearly circumscribed by the more public institutions of family, community, nation. Each individual was defined and developed as part of a series of larger groupings, and with loyalties and values that could be in conflict with those of other groups. The public dimension of human life has always been contested.

In recent times, with the rise of individual rights and identities, the seed of life has been seen increasingly as primarily a personal growth. There has been a shift towards a more reflective, self-referential approach through which the individual tends to evaluate and choose relationships around their own personal experience, rather than as part of a wider public, social role and context. Such constantly negotiated relationships are more likely to be ended if they do not quickly deliver the personal experience desired. Pace has become important, at the expense of patience and stability. Rather than faith in what has been given, the emphasis has become placed on an agency that can deliver.

This approach to relationships privileges the private over the public. There is a stronger likelihood of relationship generating greater intensity, excitement and emotional honesty, but at the cost of huge instabilities, uncertainties and stress.[1]

In terms of husbandry for the seeds of life, given this shift in climate, there are three interesting traditions of cultivation. The first can be identified with the French Revolution of 1789 (reinforced by those of 1830 and 1840) which places the emphasis firmly upon freedom and progress. There have been huge benefits in terms of freedom of thought, commerce, communication. The doctrine of individual rights has steadily been offered to every citizen, especially through the right to vote. Yet, in practice, such freedom has consistently been available only to a minority, and the pressures of pluralism have been handled through the competition of the market. Law has become an umpire, but secures only a basic stability, within which huge inequalities flourish. Thus both the individual and society become subject to forces of stress which seem to bring some benefits amongst huge uncertainty and unevenness. The watchword becomes insecurity and the outcome becomes stress. The primary power is that of freedom.

The second tradition for the cultivation of the seeds of human life can be associated with the Roman model of empire – both political and ecclesiastical. The focus is not freedom for each individual to be negotiated and exploited. Rather the emphasis is upon the prior privilege of belonging to a more public (catholic) reality which requires duty and service as primary concerns – rather than liberty and success. This model is indicative of a vast, carefully ordered context – society and eventually eternity. The emphasis is less on pace to deliver immediate satisfactions, and more on fidelity to an established wisdom and ethos that gathers up every personal pathway into an ever unfolding mystery of goodness and grace.

Within this second model, the seed of individual life grows not so much through external works of achievement, but within. The inner energy of the seed is part of a divine energy rising continually within creation to nourish lives called to fulfilment in another key – in eternity. In this model the public element has priority: parts are given life to serve the Body. Stress will be no longer be seen as frustrating dysfunction, but rather will be recognised as a normative ingredient of each part or life, constantly adjusting to discern and fulfil its commitment to a much greater enterprise. The primary power is no longer the assertion of freedom – it becomes the acceptance of authority: faithfulness.

A third frame for the husbandry of the human seeds of life is a more hybrid approach associated with an English constitutional monarchy.

This frame has given significant space to the development of individual freedom, particularly in terms of political participation. Nonetheless the problems of continuing inequality beneath the rhetoric and the rights awarded to individuals has continued. However, this trajectory towards freedom for all individuals has been tempered by owning a prior authority in a Monarch – who represents the whole and who authorises the endeavours of people to order freedom. The weight has been upon the value of tradition, precedent and what has been already established. There has been a strong emphasis upon continuity and catholicity, as well as space for radical experiment and exploration. The constitutional and democratic framework places tradition, law and established wisdom in a dynamic with debate, further possibilities and means of negotiated development or change. Freedom and faith are framed in a continuing dynamic.

Despite the widespread recognition of the merits of this model of constitutional democracy across the so called western world, there seems increasingly a shifting towards the French Revolution Model of privileging the notion of unbridled freedom for the individual, reinforced by the spread of globalisation and the priority of a market led approach. Yet the trappings of public ritual, deference and a deep seated patriotism in some, have served to keep something of this more balancing dynamic alive. In the United Kingdom it has been more clearly preserved in the Church of England, since the Gospel of the unique preciousness and freedom of every human life is held more clearly within an Establishment of prior authority, ritual and tradition, placed in every community as a sign and invitation to taste and participate in this kind of ever-including dynamic.

However, both the English nation and the Anglican Church face a serious moment of testing in the present climate where there is a growing tension between individual claims for freedom and institutionalised power blocks organising ever greater control, whether through market mechanisms such as Google or Amazon, or through narrower political movements such as populism and the growth of 'top down' government as modelled by China, Singapore or Dubai – mirrored in the church by the new roles assumed by increasingly impatient and vociferous parties.

As 'freedom' has become a claim for space for the self, reinforcing a signal that each seed must fend for itself, the focus has been upon the material manifestation of immediate desires. The short termism highlighted by the speed of communication and the desire for instant response has increased stress and reduced aspiration to very low levels. The growth of pornography and internet dating take increasing precedence over the mysteries of trying to build and maintain long term relationships.

And yet there is a growing awareness of the significance of the environment – both as a long-term project endangered by the short-termisms of individual freedom, and as a much more complex and delicate connecting context than has been hitherto recognised. Concern for the environment marks a possible return to a deeper awareness of being part of a larger project than the time span of an individual life, and an awareness of the need to try to discern the deeper currents and workings of the world in which we are set. Those who acknowledge the environmental challenge stand on the threshold of owning the smallness of creatures before the mysterious majesty of the Creator.

In this context, there needs to be a greater emphasis upon discernment, cooperation and mutuality. New models of husbandry for the seeds of human life will need to move beyond the political (and religious) poles that have grown so powerfully around liberty or authority – freedom or fundamentalism. These extreme emphases both deliver stress and frustration while promising wholeness and satisfaction.

We are poised on the brink of a challenge to re-emphasis the centrality of the dynamic within each life, and between lives, in terms of independence and dependence, uniqueness and connectivity. This essential complexity within the seeds of life must be nourished by a renewed engagement with the One who gives life – the living purpose and presence of Father, Son and Holy Spirit; the Giver of the triple gift.

In such a context the Italian prophet Mazzini came to see that the key to an appropriate care for the seed of life was not the apparently obvious task of politics – that is appropriate organisation of nourishment and development – a path which has tended to dominate both political and religious endeavours. Rather the most important element should be what he termed 'mysticism'.[2] Politics, religion, art, commerce, needed to recognise the crucial role of 'an overworld', a Heaven'. The fundamental problem with the modern world was that it was unheavened.

And of course seeds require warmth and light from beyond. Forces for goodness that can be seen and tasted (experienced) but not controlled. Heaven offers a sign not only of a much more vast project within which human life is unfolding, but also a sign of greater powers that engage with earthly living, for good and ill, without clear communication or any obvious accountability. Humanity has the sense of looking up to Heaven, and being looked down upon.

The mystic knows the reality of being 'wrong' and deeply dependent. There is a desire to look towards a greater, essentially mysterious authority, and yet a recognition of the responsibility of each seed to grow according to the purposes of its Creator. Thus freedom could never be mistaken for achievement, but only as an invitation to play a humble part in a greater endeavour whose purpose would always be beyond human comprehension.

The structures and values crystallised by human wisdom would provide tested markers, but be always subject to further revelation. The mystic takes seriously what has been given, but always as a sign of what is to come. Thus prayer and the public liturgy are defining sites of thanksgiving, humble offering and further call and commission. Temples for the offering of sacrifice and the receiving of blessing.

This mystical approach is the crucial antidote to the temptation to make an idol of particular human experience or achievements, which becomes a recipe for conflict since perceptions are so diverse, according to context, aptitude and conditioning. Freedom claimed for immediate purposes becomes a recipe for conflict. The mystic sees freedom as an opportunity to give priority to Heaven – and thus to bring duty and service to the fore of organisation and valuing of the human endeavour.

In practical terms this prioritising of the mystical would recast the 'freedoms' claimed through democracy from an agglomeration of voters seeking the immediate welfare of themselves, to a society of believers – an association of lives linked by a common duty to discernment, discipline and devotion. The agenda then shifts from balancing competing claims towards reconciling human hearts through common ownership of a connecting spirit and a shared context. A 'spirituality' equipped to live with and through the messiness and contradictions of the human journey.

A touchstone of this dilemma in modern society would be the place of the 'family'. The forces of freedom and the increase of mobility have combined to put severe pressure upon the family, and much evidence shows disintegration or constant renegotiation. Moreover the claims of 'equal marriage' can be seen to be extending towards alliances with a number of partners, rather than the traditional two. Many children are seeds developed outside of such a stable environment, and thus suffer the stress of feeling responsible for their own survival and flourishing.

Yet the family is not only the site which produces the 'seeds' of life – it has been recognised across all cultures as the key 'public' place for maturing development.

This site of nourishment places individual 'freedom' within the prior context of responsibility towards the whole – as a microcosm for wider expressions of public life. Families work not just through clearly reasoned policies, but within a web of inherited tradition, unspoken bonds of affection, and a deeper sense of a shared journey. These realities are expressed through rituals, 'liturgies of word and deed', and a sense of responsibility which acknowledges the internal and the external contexts. The key is participation, not particular performance.

The same factors apply to religion as an essentially 'family' phenomenon. The rational individualised world concentrates upon the defining significance of personal beliefs and their relevance in various contexts, reducing religion to an 'expressive, individual presentation of feelings stripped of any collective relevance'.[3] The result is that diversity is addressed in terms of sentiment, with no recognition of deeper connecting currents and callings to participation in a common life within a shared environment.

The outcome is a continuing disintegration of culture and disconnectivity of personal experience and identities. Freedom becomes the right to be in the present, rather than the potential to be drawn into an unfolding and only dimly perceived future. The preservation of the seed becomes the agenda, rather than the possibility of transformation into something very different, and completely organic – participation into the flow of eternity. The difference between accommodation of existing entities and participation in the salvation of the world is vital.

Thus Christian witness must beware of the temptations towards self-preservation that might seem to be achievable by negotiated adjustment to liberal democratic culture, or a confined space within a more dictatorial regime. Instead Christian witness is called to express this deeper current of participation, and ever invite people into the mystical reflective space of sacramental worship and prayer. The outworkings, as St Paul recognised, will be much more akin to the dutiful culture of Roman citizenship, and wary of the grand claims of human wisdom promising a personalised freedom.

In 2006 Pope Benedict recognised this core calling of 'the protection and promotion of the dignity of the person'[4] – but always within the organic structures of the Family and the Church. Both are spaces of intimacy where organic connectivity with creation can be given freedom within a frame of primary mutuality. Because any one person does not choose those with whom they are thus connected, these relationships should be seen as gifts to be treasured. The first response should always be thanks – Eucharist: whatever the challenges and costs of the sacrifices involved.

Thus the key remains intimate relationship as the clue to inhabiting and operating institutional arrangements. Reflection on the inner life will be a surer guide than measurement of external manifestations. The latter lead to laws - the former remains open to the fluid unpredictability of love. Silence is important, as is the perspective of other voices, especially those parts of the body which are easily neglected or ignored.

Life is called into a continuing conversation which works by silence and listening, as much as by words and positive expression. Seeds grow secretly – the inner is key to determining the outer.

Endnotes

[1] A. Giddens, Modernity and Self-Identity, CUP 1991.

[2] G.O. Griffiths: Mazzini : Prophet of Modern Europe, Fertig 1970, p66.

[3] Ed. E Uitz, Religion in the Public Square, Eleven 2011, p35.

[4] Ibid, p97.

৶ 6 ৼ

Anglican Sustenance:

Association and Outreach

Anglicanism embraces a number of sources of sustenance and forms of participation. The formal origin in the sixteenth and seventeenth centuries was distinguished by a retreat into a form of isolationism. Oxford and Cambridge ceased to be the centres of European learning that they had been in medieval times, and eventually were only open to those who subscribed to the Thirty-nine articles. The agenda of the church matched that of the nation. A particular form of organic operation, highlighted by the pressures of parties and movements within politics as within a national church.

From the beginning there was a recognition that the reality of unity was constantly tested by the fact of complexity. Life would proceed from a dynamic to be lived but never fully mastered.

By the eighteenth century, the response of the Anglican Church to the Enlightenment 'Age of Reason' was an explosion of evangelical religion, beginning with an appeal to individual feeling and decision making, and growing into a thirst for a knowledge that could offer the gospel with clarity. As a result society was seen in terms of a social contract, to be recognised and accepted, rather than as an organism growing secretly. Utilitarianism seemed to be a common sense expression of incarnation. Scientific confidence in measurement was becoming the mark of 'truth' and therefore of policy and practice.

Theologically the emphasis was upon the Atonement as a mechanism transacting salvation. The doctrine of the Trinity was relegated into the obscure background of early Christianity.

Within this trajectory of development, the spirit of a growing scientific culture, individual feeling and identity was secured within larger schemes of understanding and organisation. Deism and industrial revolution.

Eventually the Oxford movement pointed towards the neglected area of 'Reserve'.[1] A silent awe before the saving mystery of a love given freely and generously. The emphasis shifted from a focus upon the Epistles – as the resource for building both church and society – to the Gospels as the resource for placing all these important endeavours within the mystery of a coming Kingdom, met primarily "within". Here lay the secret source of owning a commitment to a covenant, which was far more subtle than composing contracts for more immediate application.

These different emphases within the Anglican enterprise should not be taken to be alternatives. They are varying manifestations of a core church settlement secured in the Declaration of Assent commitment, made by formal officeholders, to an ecclesiastical body which will always be 'one, holy, catholic and apostolic.' Within this complex dynamic of traditions, identities and aspirations, four key resources can be identified: scripture, creeds, sacraments and the historic episcopate.[2]

This kernel of identities and resources will always provoke a dynamic of change and challenge. There can be no settled pattern of life – but only a journey. This Gospel momentum works by unsettling both church and civic communities, and points to markers for future development hidden in those who have been hitherto marginalised or excluded.

Hence there should be a wariness of any emphasis upon unity or reconciliation. The eating of the Lord's flesh and the drinking of His blood are indicators of destruction opening up new life: a counter cultural approach to sustenance. Thus the art of the church is to offer shaping for unshaping. Crucifixion is a method of interruption of the apparent flow of life. There remains a deep instinct to cultivate external conformity and inner coherence, as a means of guarding against the sheer, radical destructivity of this strange kind of sustenance. The temptation is always to negotiate patterns of dependability rather than risk pathways to be pursued in hope.

Primacy must be given to the deed done in Jesus Christ, and renewed in the Eucharist celebration. It ensures that the church is primarily a place where sinners gather under the cross – united in missing the mark and falling short, yet being able to share supper with the Lord. Even Simon the Pharisee – who loved little – was able to share in this including table fellowship. Thus the Eucharist is not an individual experience, but always a divine action, through which sinners are blessed into fellowship through the Spirit of Self Sacrificial gift. The invitation is to those who know that they are wrong: "those who are well have no need of a physician, but those who are sick; I have come to call not the righteous but sinners" (Mark 2[17]).

Christ's continuing availability to the needs of sinners reshapes the meaning of His humility, and of our discipleship. It is for this reason that B. F. Westcott was so positive about the sustenance which the Church of England was called to offer. Her legal status ensured that the Church should offer points of contact for all: through public worship and the occasional offices of baptism, weddings and funerals. These offers stemmed from an unbroken connection with the growing of the seeds implanted through the Gospel and made manifest in various stages of the history of the Church – both East and West – signified by 'the jealous maintenance of the historic episcopate'[3], and the 'affinity with the non-episcopal churches of the Reformation by its appeal to the Scriptures as containing all things that are required of necessity to salvation.'

Like the giving of the original sustenance in flesh and blood, this ministry proceeds by a process of laying aside as well as of assimilation, because 'those most sharply separated from one another by their circumstances and by their forms of thought have yet within them the same principle of eternal life'.[4]

This deeper, inner unity cannot be defined, but it can be expressed through the Truth in action, a common endeavour for public service. In this sense the form of sustenance, as sacrificial giving of the very self, means that re-formation will be a continuing process, not a one-off event.

In practice this catholic, including, commission was enshrined through the establishment of dioceses and parishes to reflect a foundation in the inclusivity of the Creator's gifting of life, as a guard against the drift into more exclusive spaces seeking settlement rather than journeying into the unknown. This is why use of the vernacular has been so central. Not simply a matter of enabling better communication by shifting from the Latin language to English, but more, an invitation for every voice to be included in the dialogue of liturgy, involving human souls in the unfolding of divine goodness.

For these reasons Anglicanism has never been a 'membership' church accessed by joining, and thus fulfilling certain criterion. Rather, the Church of England assumes membership unless people choose to leave or stay away. Each person is free to make their own decision.

As a result the Church of England has always expressed its witness through a generous philanthropy alongside an including invitation into public worship. This stems from a concern for public values and welfare, as an essential counterpart to rightly ordered worship and believing.

In the eighteenth century this agenda was addressed through the development of voluntary associations, consecrating commitment to goodness through expressing this inner calling within structures of friendship and mutuality – both for the direct participants, and for those to whom they tried to offer positive nourishment – something of themselves and their own resources.

As an industrial revolution gathered pace around strategies for accumulation and a distribution based upon capacity to pay or purchase, the National Church was developing a counter ecology of gracious giving for the sake of enabling goodness in others, ie. those being wronged by the emerging systems, especially those experiencing lack.[5] The Church developed an economy of gift, over and against the economy of balancing exchange and measurable rewards. Much of this initiative came from the zeal and diligence of the clergy. Leadership felt a responsibility for both the wellbeing of the gathering institution of the Church, and for those being excluded by the prevalent forces of society.

The outcome was collaboration 'in the conception, cultivation and promotion of an array of new institutions, many of them with little or no precedent ... devoted to moral and religious oversight, confessional expression and charitable relief'.[6] There were societies for mission, for the reformation of manners, a charity school movement and numbers of relief agencies. The sustenance experienced within the church through the sacrificial mystery of the Eucharist was enacted into the surrounding society. Sacrifice of self, connected to a similar commitment in others, creating an energy for sharing this joining love more widely.

Those endeavours sowed the seeds of a voluntary cooperation that was to flower in the late nineteenth century as Christian socialism. Subsequent moves to professionalise this kind of outreach have undermined the depth of the nourishment involved. Love has been turned into measured service, and the spiritual connectivity between all concerned has been replaced by a more negotiated approach to achieving more limited aims. In the original voluntary associations there was a recognition of mutuality that owned a radical oneness, as was evidenced in the ability of recipients of care to become involved in its administration.[7]

Thus the witness of the church was able to offer sustenance to the growth of social and cultural programmes, enabled through a wave of organisational experimentation. The London Magazine of 1767 described such endeavours as being 'for relieving distress, encouraging merit, promoting virtue and propagating religion'.[8] The free flow of conversation in the new public space of the coffee-house provided an important seeding ground, alongside the more circumspect space of prayer and liturgy. The Gospel was active in both areas since they were a natural complement to one another. It is a pity that coffee after Church has become so de-politicised!

The Church of England invested these voluntary endeavours with a sense of sacred calling and holy nourishment for all who might participate. The aim was not conversion to a particular, closed way of life, nourished through its own special sources. Rather the whole endeavour was to encourage the offering of love into a public realm of competing and overlapping societies within a single society seeking the pathways to greater fulfilment. Against an age of increasing empire and globalisation, there was confidence in the muddle and plurality of localised endeavours towards goodness.

As this scenario unfolded, observance of formal religion was declining, but the energy of love continued to flow. The consecration of the 'civic' shifted attention away from the ecclesiastical: though the common roots and values remained important factors enabling an essential cohesion and continuity. Eventually the need for confessional renewal would become apparent, so that the source of sustenance could be maintained. The failure to ensure such a renewal has led to a disconnection between much voluntary charity and regular church life. It is only as the more professionalised service of the welfare state is dissolving under the pressure of self-concern across society expressed in an almost universal desire not to pay taxes, that an opportunity may be reappearing which will create space for love as sacrificial self-giving for the sake of the needs of others.

With the demise of big systems and a demand for local, personal, contextual engagement, there is an important opportunity for a renewal of such an associational, entrepreneurial and improvising style of outreach into the real agendas of struggling lives. Such outreach is not only the proper manifestation of Christian discipleship formed out of the body and blood of Christ, but it also offers such divine sustenance through the sharing of a spirit of selfless mutuality. Just as Jesus shifted Jewish religious practice into the streets and by-ways, beyond the control of the 'ecclesiastical', so we can re-learn how the gospel can become a liberating power in ways not anticipated by church systems.

Thus the gospel unfolds through dual paths of participation: within the Eucharistic community, and through the love captured and shared by voluntary associations. The more formal public realm will often threaten these forums for sustenance, but needs to be challenged and reminded to accept and employ them gratefully. As St Paul recognised, in Romans 13, public authority has a particular role in providing the framework within which spiritual and material nourishment can be created and shared.

Society needs this important interplay between the specific focus of the Last Supper and its more general offering through fellowship around meals and works of goodness. Such Sacred Service needs freedom for initiative and thus a certain independence from the control of the state. The Church becomes a gathering and a distributive agency of the love that issues in the life of creation.

Endnotes

[1] Isaac Williams. Tract 80 and 87: On Reserve in Communicating Religious Knowledge, 1838:1840.

[2] Alastair Redfern. Being Anglican, DLT 2000.

[3] B. F. Westcott, Christian Aspects of Life, Macmillan 1901, p70.

[4] Ibid, p74.

[5] Ed. S. Padover. The Essential Marx, Mentor, 1978, p93.

[6] S. Sisiton, The Christian Monitor, Yale, 2014, p4.

[7] Alastair Redfern, The Clewer Initiative, ISPCK 2017.

[8] S. Sisiton, The Monitor, Yale, 2014, p6.

ॐ 7 ॐ

From Dust to Dust:

The Cost of Growth

The ideals which love illuminates are easily reduced to systems of boundaries which can exclude and cause suffering. A powerful example would be the story of the woman taken in adultery (John 8[1-11]). The ideals of faithfully committed marital relations, and the failure for these ideals to be observed, can become the cause of judgement, condemnation and death.

While Jesus went to the Mount of Olives. Early in the morning he came again to the temple. All the people came to him and he sat down and began to teach them. The scribes and the Pharisees brought a woman who had been caught in adultery; and making her stand before all of them, they said to him, "Teacher, this woman was caught in the very act of committing adultery. Now in the law Moses commanded us to stone such women. Now what do you say?" They said this to test him, so that they might have some charge to bring against him. Jesus bent down and wrote with his finger on the ground. When they kept on questioning him, he straightened up and said to them, "Let anyone among you who is without sin be the first to throw a stone at her." And once again he bent down and wrote on the ground. When they heard it, they went away, one by one, beginning with the elders; and Jesus was left alone with the woman standing before him. Jesus straightened up and said to her, "Woman, where are they? Has no one condemned you?" She said, "No one, sir." And Jesus said, "Neither do I condemn you. Go your way, and from now on do not sin again." John 8 (1-11)

Jesus intervenes in this apparently simple administration of justice by digging deeper – into the dust. Each person present, whether righteous or sinful, is formed from that dust. There is a basic commonness in life. No-one is 'pure', all are dirtied as dust. The foundation for community is a gracious forgiveness and humility. Each person is always wrong. This is an important starting place. It does not excuse sin, but it provides an important holding framework.

The relativity of experience tends to conceal an underlying universal reality – and it is the latter which is the only foundation for social and community life. A moral community is formed not by simple behavioural conformities, but only by engaging with a common spiritual foundation. A society which owns that it is fundamentally organic, dealing with the mysteries of difference and the apparently contradictory behaviours and values of the various elements. Ownership of this mystery would enable a graciousness that looks upon sin, as missing the mark, with creative compassion, amidst a deeper desire to give the self into the service of better possibilities, and a commitment to contributing with others, through such distressing challenges, towards a common good.

In the story, the 'sin' is not endorsed, but the response is deeper than the merely reciprocal exchange of an economic approach. Of course there will need to be deterrence and punishment, but these are not ends in themselves – rather they must be always part of this more including approach. In inviting the woman caught in adultery to sin no more, Jesus was offering a new opportunity to move from always being wrong, of the dust, towards a richer set of possibilities in a redeemed Eucharistic (thanksgiving) community where justice conceived as rights and offences against those rights, is replaced by a humble acceptance of God's righteousness – gifted into our fallen wrongness. This insight must not encourage the response which St Paul faced – that we should therefore sin so that God's grace may abound (Romans 6[1]). Such a view is merely a way of re-expressing a basic economic transaction approach of measureable outcomes and rewards.

Rather the woman taken in adultery is offered as a sign of how her being in the wrong can be met not through any effort or achievement of her own, nor through over simplistic, self-preserving judgment by others, but simply by having the humility to accept an unmerited and unexpected gift of grace. Love conquering all that is less than love, and thus able to indwell the unworthy in order to make us agents of a love beyond our control or comprehension.

Hegel in The Phenomenology of The Spirit used the image of the life of a plant.

> 'The bud disappears in the bursting-forth of the blossom, and one might say that the former is refuted by the latter; similarly, when the fruit appears, the blossom is shown up in its turn as a false manifestation of the plant, and the fruit now emerges as the truth of it instead. These forms are not just distinguished from one another, they also supplant one another as mutually incompatible. Yet at the same time their fluid nature makes them moments of an organic unity in which they not only do not conflict, but in which each is as necessary as the other, and this mutual necessity alone constitutes the life of the whole'.[1]

The point is that our 'experience' and aspiration at any one time have to be trusted into a totality whose general sense of direction we can glimpse, but whose inner workings only give an intimation of what might be to come. This indicates the proper role of the institution, as the frame for holding the truth of the totality, the vision and promise of Heaven, while stewarding the rituals and sacraments given to enable appropriate engagement on the way. The aim is to represent the possibilities and to minister into their implications — especially the challenge to seeking a more stable security in present beliefs or practices.

Officers of the institution exercise leadership to mediate between people, contexts, values and interpretations. This priestly work emerges not from analysis and knowledge, but from the gentle advocacy of forgiveness and love as practiced by Our Lord with the woman taken in adultery. Thus leadership will not be primarily about adhering to established codes, but rather the emphasis will always be on inviting an engagement through which blossom may grow into something beyond. An echo of Jesus's word that He comes not to judge the world at any one point of time, which was the expectation of both religious and political leaders of His time. Rather He comes to save the world – to bring to birth fuller health and flourishing. The aim is to raise sights, not crush expectations.

A church witnessing to such a gospel will operate through the outflow of the love that it is gifted to receive, and the most appropriate vehicle of this mission will be 'voluntary associations' – which would include the family as a primary model for energizing freedom within a framework of deep mutuality. There will be only a supportive and penultimate place for systems. The role of the church as institution is to oversee but renew the necessary systems of ordering that enable life, but all too easily slide into oppressive forms of limitation and judgement.

The approach will work through a continuing attempt to synthesise without putting too much weight upon analysis.

Exercising judgement can provide important focus and shaping, but it must always accept an inbuilt tendency to be 'wrong' in the sense of only being a small part of a much greater totality. This dynamism needs to be mystical in its commitment to engaging equally with experience, silence, waiting and receiving moments of shaping visitation – since there is the potential for being drawn more deeply into the possibility of perfection (full fruition) for every creature.

Each person and context needs to be able to develop these reflective, attentive capacities – a paying attention to the dust as a primary and foundational response to every challenge and disappointment. The dust is a reality which prevents strict demarcation between individuals, groups and society or between those adjudged in human terms as righteous or wicked. Such 'divisions' are held within the institutional arrangements of the Church, which privilege 'sinners' and call for common conformity to being always 'wrong'.

Although political activities will, of necessity, have to work with firmer boundaries, and moments of more decisive civic judgments, the distinctive role of the church is to stand in a different place offering a forgiving, encouraging and consecrating ministry to saint and sinner alike. This is the true catholicity of the Gospel, which cannot be contained by human systems. There is an understandable need to build on the dust, but construction soon imitates the Tower of Babel, and the taking up of those of the dust into the mystery of heaven requires a very different kind of sustenance and ministration.

Therefore the Church presumes a basic unity, and a common spirit that grace can infuse with growth towards goodness. This highlights the purpose of power within creation to be concerned with the process of the bud and the blossom, rather than a simple ordering of what might seem to be righteousness at any one juncture. Beneath every endeavour is the dust of primeval creation. Justice unfolds as a dynamic, rather than a static exercise, and 'judgements' need to be developmental rather than imply more definitive outcomes. A good judicial system recognises that there can always be further evidence which will change perspectives and possibilities. Such evidence will not be merely material, through the unfolding of the stuff of creation. Rather new evidence is primarily arising through the purifying of the soul and a greater openness to the triple gift which delivers the grace of God. Dust needs the atmosphere of a divine climate to enable good life to grow.

Such a process can never be characterised as developmental, since the experience of some elements and participants will appear to be negative rather than positive – only to be redeemed within the fullness of humanity. In Hegel's imagery, the blossom falls, but nonetheless plays a crucial part.

The same wisdom needs to be applied to our awareness of societies and social organisations – each of which are tempted to assume a kind of superiority in their identity and in their endeavours. In fact the basic call to humility and openness is equally applicable – but it is much more difficult to invite and enable this spiritual activity in large scale organisations. This is why the church has an important role as a model of possible alternatives – but also a function in reminding organisations of their frailty, limitation, and need for love as well as service if the process of fruition is to be able to flow through bodies corporate.

The Eucharistic sharing of peace is a sign of how limitation and variety in individuals and in the organisations they represent, can be connected in a gesture of goodwill full of the most radical political and social responsibilities.

Societies, like individuals need to grasp a sense of wonder and a faith in the largeness of the project of human being.

Thus the inculcation of a public spirit is an important political, societal responsibility, and the church has a contribution in offering occasions for its manifestation – the ability to mix hope with mourning, and failure with forgiveness. Such a spirituality reproduces itself through permeating boundaries and connecting in commonness.

At a time when communal solidarities are dissolving, there is a tendency for public, social organisation to seek justification in rationalised systems of 'service'. In fact individual aspirations need a more imaginative and including framework, within which hearts can hope for Heaven and difficulties can be transformed into healing. Such an agenda is the work of love, and our key challenge is how to enable social arrangements to make space for this life-enhancing power.

These challenges to worldly forms of organisation present an important missionary moment through which the church can focus not upon obstacles to a successful presentation of the faith, which is the tendency of much Apologetic – but rather there opens up a vast common ground between church and world. An identical agenda, and strong signs of deep, spiritual resources that act across more superficial divisions and priorities. The task is to identify a common concern for growth in human lives that is not tied narrowly to organisational arrangements and values, but which can be explored through creative working with the real concerns of individuals and groups in terms of the perplexing unevenness of life, the frustrations of limitations to health and wellbeing, and the deep desire for wholeness and glory.

Edward Caird expressed this challenging opportunity in a Lay Sermon in Balliol College Chapel in 1896 when he quoted Tennyson: 'we must look to the Christ that is, and the Christ that is to be ... as the centre of our hopes for humanity'.[2]

Such a vision can form the basis of an attempt 'to reinterpret experience in the light of a unity which is presupposed in it': 'the unity of all things with each other, and with the mind that knows them'.[3] Such participation becomes the source of both morality and religion: the path for each person and the participation which can give true trajectory to our different forms of political and social organisation.

Thus the dualisms and binaries so prevalent in the confrontation with the woman taken in adultery are in fact elements that each include something of the other: the common component of the dust. Bishop Butler opposed the competitive individualism identified by Thomas Hobbes with the observation that, in fact, 'the indications that we are made for society ... and to do good to our fellow creatures'[4] are equally prevalent and available for appropriate response.

Endnotes

[1] J Stewart, Idealism and Existentialism, Continuum 2010, p28.

[2] H. Jones & J Muirhead, The Life and Philosophy of Edward Caird, Macmillan 1921, p149.

[3] Ibid, p150.

[4] J.R. Illingworth, Divine Transcendence, Macmillan 1911, p77.

❧ 8 ❧

Showing the Way:

Leadership and the Ministry of Meditation

Leadership in such a testing environment has been identified in the Church of England with episcopacy. An example of the fundamental mixture of firmness and flexibility required in such a role would be the approach of Samuel Wilberforce, Bishop of Oxford in the nineteenth century, at a time of considerable tensions between different factions in the church, together with the emergence of more established political parties in the life of the State, and an alarming growth of poverty and dispossession as the hidden outcomes of the public projects of the Industrial Revolution and the growing of Empire.

Wilberforce oversaw the development of religious orders in his diocese. An innovation since the abolition of the monasteries in the sixteenth century Reformation which produced the Church of England. His support for the sisterhood established at Clewer, near Windsor, raised considerable opposition from the established protestantism of much of the Church of England. Moreover the sisters developed views about taking vows and religious obedience which Wilberforce resisted.[1] However he recognised the realities of the complex challenges thus presented into the church, stating in his charge of 1869 that he could not 'stand aloof from any who were bent on doing the work of Christ within the Church of England, even though there were in their way of doing it, certain things of which I did not myself altogether approve'. He goes on : 'it has always appeared to me to be the duty of a bishop in the English Church to throw himself heartily, without stint or grudgingly into the labours of the clergy or laity of all the different schools of thought, which are allowed within her communion.'[2]

Clearly there will be boundaries, and judgements to be made, but within the sphere of all labouring for Christ he will offer support 'by his prayers, his personal cooperation and his confidence.' This approach was certain to involve great difficulties and suspicion from 'the narrow minded', with accusations of 'a want of care for absolute truth' and 'a sinful desire to please men.'

The task of the bishop, of leadership as oversight, is to 'live down such suspicions', upholding all that 'the church has received as vital of dogmatic truth' but allowing 'for large differences of tone, of feeling, and of the mode of expressing the common faith'. Thus there needed to be a 'permitted variance' through which 'the main sides of the common truth will be most faithfully maintained in themselves, and most readily supplied for the spiritual sustenance of others.' He believed that 'all life, because it is life, has of necessity this faculty of diversity or reproduction qualified with essential unity.'[3]

Leadership is to oversee the allowing of variety within recognised limits – the gift of love has an integrity but also an overflowing creativity. Wilberforce aimed to be bishop not of a party but of a diocese. Leadership was not about a judicious handling of power. Rather it required a commitment to oversee creative interchange between different elements voluntarily inhabiting a common framework. There was an important role in ensuring the maintenance of some kind of framework, consonant with the values and direction of the individual gift.

Further, this approach to leadership, like that of the Good Shepherd, involves a pro-active effort to recognise and include the hidden contributions of countless ordinary people whose faith, generosity and idealism is not caught up in particular 'party' efforts, but who nonetheless serve to be conduits of a continuing flow of goodness and grace for the sake of others. The institutionalisation of organisation has a tendency to exclude this hidden economy, and concentrate upon the more formalised actors and agencies.

In fact many ordinary human actions are gladly cooperative and assume a degree of goodness in others: whether walking across a zebra crossing or entrusting oneself to a provider of food or drink. We tend to assume safety or nourishment rather than injury or poisoning! Such motives are important determinants of actions. Yet too often leadership looks to performance and its management, rather than into the hearts and secrets of others seeking goodness but experiencing certain amounts of darkness or frustration.

Jesus issues the challenge 'why call me good?' (Mark 10[18]). Only One is good, and human living is the privilege of being invited to participate in that goodness. An example would be St Paul's approach to the slavery which was a key part of the workings of his contemporary society. He did not launch an outright attack from a superior moral high ground. Instead he invited deeper reflection about attitudes. Masters should not threaten; slaves should serve masters as of serving Christ; Philemon should receive back Onesimus not as a slave, but as a beloved brother. Here was the germ of attitudes which had the potential to transform inner lives and their translation into everyday practice. Institutional reform was to take centuries, but the seeds were sown and the possibility of ameliorative and healing practice was established.

This is an instance of leadership that invites into the complexities of which Samuel Wilberforce was so aware, and encouraged the outflow of transformative love, even though formal economic and social systems were to prove initially, impervious to any organisational expression of such values. Interestingly it was Samuel Wilberforce's father, William Wilberforce, who had found an appropriate institutional way of privileging such basic Christian attitudes in relation to slavery. The connecting thread was leadership attuned to the primacy of the inner life and its nourishment through grace:

highlighted by his work with the Clapham Sect. This will always be the engine room of morality and societal blessing.

Charles Gore captured something of this commission in his book "The Social Doctrine of the Sermon on the Mount" when he stated that 'the church is not to represent public opinion, but to be the home of the best moral conscience of the community".[4]

This style of leadership would fail to meet many modern criteria. In the model of Jesus there was no sense of Strategic Public Relations. People asked him to give signs but much of his leadership was done in secrecy, and with an alarming inconsistency by the standards of efficient human organisation.

It is against this background that we must evaluate the fact that according to worldly criteria the church continues to be 'visibly disappointing' (Gore). The Church offers a ministry of the promise of the triple gift of love – but its delivery and its effectiveness are a mystery beyond her own control. As a human institution indwelt by the Holy Spirit, the 'performance' of the church will be uneven yet faithful to the power of promise. The leadership and ministry of Jesus would earn the same evaluation by worldly standards. Dust never seems the best material from which to bring forth new life.

In St Paul tensions and divisions are the very stuff of leadership, and of the life of the church, as his letters to the Corinthians makes explicit. In the relationship with the Galatians too, leadership works with and through the

divisions of the church and the disagreements of society.
There is no simple path of purity and love.

At the Church Congress in Oxford in 1862 Bishop
Samuel Wilberforce offered a forceful articulation of this
role of leadership and ecclesiastical organisation. He told
his audience that

> "*there will always be subjects on which good men, from
> the mere natural laws of the mind contemplating one
> side of the subject more continually and with greater
> interest than another, will come to somewhat different
> conclusions: and on these subjects manifestly it is of
> the greatest use that men who are in earnest, men who
> are thoughtful, men who have one common object,
> although they would work for that common object by
> somewhat different means, should from time to time
> consult together concerning common action, check their
> own individuality of views by being led to contemplate
> the view which presents itself most naturally to others,
> and in this way provide, first for greater unity of action
> towards our common objects, because 'In unity is our
> strength' and secondly, ascertaining not only how we
> may directly act better together, but ascertaining by
> that sort of communication each one wherein either
> his own view has been deficient or his own mode of
> promoting his own view wanting, that he may be able
> to complete for himself an aspect of the whole subject,
> and that he may be able to remove from his mode of
> endeavouring to promote the truth the hindrances which*

have unawares, from his own idiosyncrasies, crept in and marred his own work.[5]

He was "concerned for the promotion of the practical efficiency of the Church of England". To make a real and voluntary contribution into the stresses and complexities of the surrounding society, the church should concentrate not upon an internal agenda of shaping more finely doctrine or her own legislative framing – since the 'truths' they embodied would be emerging rather than completed. This was a challenge to each of the competing parties within his Diocese, since their respective agendas were focussed upon refining and defining beliefs and behaviours.

Instead, Wilberforce invited this jarring range of Christian testimonies to give priority to learning from each other in order better to witness to the world through generous service. The purpose of the Church Congress was not formal resolutions that would be binding upon participants, but mutual encouragement and commitment, across and through their differences. Thus the aim of congress was "to discuss together in a spirit of friendly questioning, some of the great subjects on which depends the advance of our church for her great work for God – of leavening His people, and through His people the world at large".[6]

This is why Anglican polity gives wide space for local leadership and expressions of the gospel witness appropriate to different contexts.

This model provides space for local and particular contributions around centres of commitment, within certain basic limits, and a common loyalty to a presiding episcopal oversight.

The parish system provides a set of separate and independent centres within a discipline to take counsel together, mitigate the narrowness that characterises becoming organised, and endorses combination through trusting one another ever more fully, while retaining integrity about 'our special opinions' – thus enabling more effective action than would be possible from separated and competing entities.

The marks of this style of leadership and operation will be moderation, a jealousy for Gospel integrity, and an anxiety to avoid damaging any for whom Christ has died. Therefore space must be given for widespread freedoms of thought and action focussed on purity and charity, and thus enabling a combination of resources not otherwise deployable. It is within this combination that power can be especially manifest: as the challenging variety of alliances adopted by Jesus in His own ministry clearly indicate.

This trajectory gives considerable resource to the church's call to engage with the bewildering variety of causes and conflicts. Such contribution offers the powers of personality and human flexibility for appropriate engagement, rather than more formal and structured approaches. Society is formed of living persons pursuing personal callings, indwelt at the deepest level by a common spirit, and ripe for fulfilment in a mutuality of grace.

Leadership within such an unfolding reality avoids being partisan, and tries to identify the prejudices behind passions, in the recognition that conviction can often cloud the understanding. Yet there must be the wisdom to resist the ever present temptation to cut short inquiry in a false seeking of clarity and consistency. The art of timing in terms of decision making and direction setting is crucial. When Lazarus died Jesus waited two days before responding.

It is much easier to be a leader of a party than of a diocese – that is of a totally inclusive area which will contain a huge variety of more private and partisan speculation.

The discipline of mortification is not just for individual spiritual formations but also an essential element of both leadership and of institutional life: not least because words, though a valuable contributor to truth, can often obscure the presence and power of a more mysterious spirit.

Such leadership is important because society has 'more complex laws of degeneration and re-creation'[7] than has often been acknowledged. Thus learning needs to take place through a variety of channels – many indirect and indicative rather than being part of a formal syllabus. The continuing threat of chaos requires renewed interpretation and mediation. Forces of conflict and threat need attention that is more subtle than simply seeking conformity to re-ordering. The less obvious registers of human wrong and gracious hope need space and time for interchange and exploration, as well as the necessity very often of safe containment. Revelation has a key role in human journeying and often arrives through what appears to be disruption and disordering

Such a ministry of mediation will function to challenge disruptive appetite and action by seeking engagement through a common humility and sense of mutuality. Coleridge pointed to a similar insight with his recognition that parts seek cultivation, whereas the whole requires civilisation.

Endnotes

[1] Alastair Redfern. The Clewer Initiative, ISPCK 2017.

[2] Samuel Wilberforce, Charge to the Diocese of Oxford, Parker 1869, p14.

[3] Ibid, pp16-18.

[4] C. Gore, The Social Doctrine of the Sermon on The Mount, Percival 1892.

[5] S.Wilberforce, Report of the Church Congress, 1862, p2.

[6] Ibid, p.4.

[7] B. Knight, The Idea of the Clerisy in the Eighteenth Century, Cambridge 1978, p12.

৯ 9 ৵

From Exile to Exaltation:

Truth as Servanthood

The servant or slave is generally not particularly visible. Below stairs in Victorian parlance. This is the secret place that the mystic seeks to inhabit – seeking a perspective from the realities experienced by those excluded and not able to contribute directly to human calculation and the making of social life. Simone Weil described the process of seeking such a perspective as 'de-creation': that is a decentring and emptying of the self to enable other voices of God's grace to be better heard.

The result will not be special 'feelings', but a richer connection with the actual lives of those excluded – with the proper sites of hidden love offering as yet unnoticed intimations of the call of grace: the bearers of the triple gift through the mysterious secret that is the love of God. The challenge of the parable of the sheep and the goats in Matthew chapter 25.

Thus the servant becomes so identified with the excluded, that they become the obvious person to die on behalf of the people – that is on behalf of those marginalised from Roman society, and those marginalised within that society. 'The people' has a very extended meaning. And thus 'judgement' is made by those exercising religious and political leadership: Caiaphas and Pilate.

Such a death is the clearest possible manifestation of the sense of exile that effective human societies inevitably create: especially through religious and political systems. Exile is, of course, the pathway through which God calls His people: hence the prevalence of chaos and conflict amidst signs of success.

Only such a route can clarify the necessary stepping away from the fleshpots of Egypt that represent the devices and desires of the world. Moreover the cleansing, mortifying experience of the wilderness (a regular occurrence in Jesus's own rule of life) begins to offer a different perspective for hope – not through the satisfaction of human desire, but through obedience to the inclusive grace of God for the salvation of a world damaged by such a high prevalence of missing this glorious mark because of the distractions of smaller objectives.

The calling into exile means abandoning strategy for the self and submitting to the unfavourable plans and processes of another Master – who has many other sheep too. This is made clear in the parable of the Good Shepherd in John chapter 10, especially the reference to the self-serving of the hired hand, which offers a classic instance of the kind of strategic thinking which prioritises established forms of order over the disturbing irruptions of new hopes and opportunities. In this approach systems are to shape spirit. Leadership becomes the responsibility to defend and refine boundaries which seem to be effective – not least by the modern criteria of numbers. The aim will be to keep the vast majority – 'the people' within a context of proven security and stability. Hence the political and religious wisdom of Caiaphas "it is better for one man to die then for the whole people to suffer (John 11[45-end]).

The servant or slave is the one who comes to question this perspective, not with an alternative, improved offer, but simply an invitation to live in ways which are more inclusive, especially of those whom Jesus had particularly identified as hidden and expendable.

A number of factors are worthy of special note. First, many of the ordinary people had connected with the grace that Jesus was bringing forth, and sensed the possibilities of new life for themselves and for the systems that 'held' them. They affirmed Jesus with their cries of Hosanna. Yet some doubted: uncertainty creates anxiety and some people look to faith and politics to assuage such discomfort. Thus, as tensions rose in Jerusalem through the mediation of new possibilities in the ministry of the Messiah, the people, in their anxiety, turned to the established leaders or overseers. Many of those in authority recognised the positive aspects identified by 'the people' – but also shared the alarm that such disruptive forces could bring challenging change and upheaval to the ways of living that at least seemed to be reasonably settled. Anxiety soon turns into fear.

The decision that one person should die and save all the people is made on the basis of knowledge. Caiaphas points out that in terms of the mixed views among the people and their parties, clearly 'they know nothing.' Knowledge is designed by human reason to hoover up anxieties and fears and place them within a more re-assuring context – and this task is the responsibility of authorised leadership. Servants need to know their place within the systems designed to ensure strength and stability: conveniently ignoring the costs paid by those generally kept out of sight by these apparently effective arrangements.

Given the threats of the alternatives offered through Jesus, the authority of such clearly defining knowledge is exercised: pragmatism and an accurate assessment of measurable results point to a simple 'solution' – 'it is better for one person to die' (John 11[50]) than for all the people to suffer disruption and harm. Proven power systems of organisation are designed to contain the spirit, not to give way before its disturbing impulse. This cautious, controlling, limiting approach is indicative of a strategy that could well describe much spirituality and the operation of a rule of life. It also shapes much parish life too, and is clearly manifest in the confident offers of political policies.

Jesus is seen as a disturber of proven, settled systems. This is an accurate perception. The mistake is to assume that He has a planned alternative to impose, possibly another version of the Roman hegemony which the Jews so bitterly resented.

In fact Jesus is simply inviting participation into an as yet unformed development of what has been already established. He had not come to abolish the law but to fulfil it. His offer is made through a procession: an invitation to reflect more radically on how love can be shared, and to be willing to explore richer ways of this life-giving power being structured and delivered. A procession led by a donkey is a radically counter cultural sign to all whose aim is to establish and defend systems! (Matthew 21).

Jesus's offer of this taste of salvation was even broader than Caiaphas had anticipated. It was not even for the whole nation, it was to gather all the dispersed children of God. Paul was to enflesh this vision with his acceptance of the call to bring Gentiles alongside Jews.

To maintain His servant role, as opposition solidified, under the leadership of Caiaphas, Jesus withdraws from the urban centre of settlement and systems, to a town called Ephraim, near the wilderness – the true site of the kind of perspectives that the servant of the whole of humanity advocates (John 11[54]). He remains in this place of borderland – between established civilisation and a different space for presence and engagement. The space which calls mystics and which releases the forces of a love that would rather be martyred than compromised in any way. Jesus had practiced this dynamic of being in the wilderness amidst all his worldly tasks throughout his ministry. He was deeply schooled in prioritising the perspective that this discipline so powerfully provided.

Of equal significance is the fact that 'the Passover was near' (John 11[55]). The remembrance of exile being the key connector between the 'world' of Egypt and the 'heavenly paradise' of a promised land. The irony of the proximity of this feast is that such a rich and sophisticated religion clearly contained all the ingredient it might require to fulfil a calling to be servant to the giving of God's salvation to the world. A defining and identity-giving narrative of being a pilgrim people ever processing through the realities of wilderness, from settlement to settlement.

Yet, despite the gift of this frame for receiving the grace of new life, only one perspective had prevailed: a conformity with the ways of the world which privileged organisation, clarity, authority and security. The features of permanent settlement, from which some were made secure, and most remained slaves. The underscoring influence of revelation through exile and Passover, through journeying and the unpredictability of utter dependence, was somehow lost. Thus it was better for one man to die for the people.

A sign of the irony of this re-affirmation of religion being ever made in the image of politics, was that this exiling experience of wilderness was to be celebrated by 'going up to Jerusalem' – ie. to the centre of security and organisation for the faith. Religion coming to pay homage to the ways of the world.

Yet other people went to this centre looking for Jesus. Poignantly, He was offering a different kind of Temple – His to-be-broken body – in the place of wilderness and desolation: outside the city wall. An invitation to a different kind of festival – one not enacted through the substitution of animals and representative rites, but an engagement of the soul in each believer – a participation of each person in a procession towards paradise through the reshaping of exile. A journey which all the people, as with Moses, were called to make.

Here is the root of a totally different spirituality, requiring a radically attentive style of leadership and a form of structures ever refined to enable the embrace of different callings and convictions.

The tragedy of our human condition is that in a sense, like the man in John, chapter 9, we are born blind. We need our eyes properly opened, by the One who heralds God's mercy. To receive such new light and therefore life, there needs to be both an acknowledgement and a testimony: 'I was blind and now I can see' - because the Lord touched my eyes. It was the religious leaders in this story who rightly felt threatened: could their claim to a particular clarity of vision in fact be a form of human blindness? A clue, as Jesus indicates, is in the claim.

The servant is the one who learns to acknowledge being blind. Spending time in the wilderness attunes the eyes to a very different vista, as it points the soul to a very different set of priorities. This vista and these priorities highlight our need for others, and for sustenance beyond the usual diet. The offer of flesh and blood can be seen as having a special spiritual significance. This is the germ of a credo that desires to embrace the wilderness of creation and the complexities of creatures – which can only be compressed into a manageable perspective through the processes of exile, waiting and longing to receive more than has been on offer

Here the servant is formed for the final journey of crucifixion – the fullness of the sacrifice of self that owns the thinness of the fleshy existence and the miracle of redemptive rescue through the fractures of the water and the dryness of the clay. Dust has a key part in the enscripting of grace – and the servant learns by making time to revisit the desert and the lesson that through its bareness new nourishment and growth can be received – through the very stuff of flesh and blood, offered into and blessed by grace – a procession most easily recognised by sinners, people owning their perpetually being in the wrong.

๙ 10 ๖

Truth:

Credo not Cogito

One of the key issues for the western liberal project is the increasing frailty of 'democracy', exposed by the rise of populist forces and extremist groups. The logic of a fully participatory society, based upon universal human rights and one-person-one-vote is too narrowly predicated on the sovereignty of the individual, expressed through the power of accumulation: authority is given to the majority.

As the Gospel recognises, human differences cannot be simply expressed or negotiated rationally. Other powers are at work. Thus Jesus is quite blunt about the reality of having enemies. He does not envisage a world without enemies – the complexities and limitations of human beings are too great to arrive at such a settled, peaceful state. Rather, the imperative is 'to love your enemies'. Difference handled with the triple gift of love, leaving space for new life to emerge beyond what might seem to be conceivable at present. Of course, there have to be intermediate ways of containing difference, and democracy is an important tool in this sense.

However, alongside democracy there needs to be other important tools, including leadership to focus authority, ritual to enable signs and occasions for broader moments of connectivity (for example Coronations, or United Nations Assemblies), laws to uphold workable boundaries, and opportunities for representation into the debate about a direction of travel, rather than in terms of immediate decision making. In the absence of these other elements being allowed to contribute, the fragility of the liberal democratic order and its official promulgation of 'neutrality' on so many fronts, simply gives space for particular groups and elitist institutions to effect control.

Besides encouraging a richer appreciation of the skills and responsibilities of citizenship, there is an urgent need for the cultivation of space for contemplation and an openness to revelation beyond the planned pathways of current knowledge. An emphasis upon appreciation and a honing of aspiration need not only engagement with the challenging varieties of human experience – but further, there could be much more exploration of the kind of connectivities between human hearts that occasionally manifest around the challenges of humanitarian disaster or the celebration of events such as sporting triumph. These moments of intensification can give clues to a deep potential for common life and common cause, transcending the more immediate concerns of the everyday.

This truth is especially prevalent in the Beatitudes (Matthew 6: Luke 6). Building upon the controlling and compelling structures of the Ten Commandments, Jesus shifts the focus from acts to attitudes. From 'knowledge' in terms of the observable and measurable, to 'seeing' with the eye of faith. A willingness to accept the secret workings of divine power. Thus the key is not behaviour, located in the specifics of the individual or the group, but character, as a disposition expressed through relationship. The casualties of human endeavour, expressed through poverty, hunger, mourning, are handled by a renewed appetite to receive righteousness, purity of heart and a passion for peace.

Power is not simply the effects of self-serving action, expressed in murder or adultery. Rather power is the inner disposition which can look no further than the desires of the self, or can become open to the widest of horizons – the flow of charity emanating from reception of the triple gift of love.

Law is now seen not as an expression of power, but as an indicator of the principles that can give guidance while allowing space for the mystery and miracle of forgiveness, for repentance that turns to a new direction, and for as yet unrecognised possibilities for engagement and connectivity. 'If anyone asks for your coat, give them your shirt too' (Matthew 5[40]), is not a literal injunction, but an example of an attitude that builds justice as charity that can create new hope. This is why Jesus can say 'I am the light of the world' (John 8 [12]) – a light that shines into other lives so that the possibilities of goodness can be seen and tasted.

This is an invitation to access a much softer understanding of power – as something which invites, encourages and nourishes, thus engendering a commitment that transcends the particular merits or failings in any one context, by allowing the faith and hope of a larger and more generously including spirit to prevail. In practical terms such an approach requires the development of a strong sense of duty – a commitment of the heart and of practice that is not simply a reflection of intellectual analysis and calculation. The truth about power is expressed through a process of reflection and learning, rather than finalised systems. As Gladstone said of the political task of discerning the truth, there needed to be 'trust in people, qualified by prudence'.[1] The broadest possible sympathies schooled by a desire to be continually learning virtue through the interplay of reflection and duty – the seeking for wisdom.

Paths for progression will always involve compromise, but in charity, rather than through clear cut exclusion or subjection. In terms of Christian wisdom, power is to be exercised within a sense of covenant, not as a simple matter of contractual correctness. A covenant implies an including mutuality around both task and as yet unknown possibilities. Within such committed commonness power can be both directed and corrected. The foundation is what J. S. Mill termed 'the great impulse to reflection'[2]: in Christian terms, the art of prayer.

Truth emerges into power as we accept the necessity of living in a world that others have made, and yet 'thinking' out our possible contribution to a continuing common life. Therefore, combinations will never be symmetrical in terms of power: such a false expectation has been the downfall of many political schemes.

George Elliott expressed this factor quite clearly in a letter in 1860 – 'man will never know the whole of his moral condition, any more than the whole of his physical or social condition. But that is not because such realities are unfavourable. It is simply that there is too much to know'.[3] Alongside the Victorian optimism about progress, there is a sharp observation about the limits of human powers, and the need to take such a fact into account when seeking the truth amidst the realities of power. Duty is the means of becoming schooled in this 'disinterested performance of self' (T.H. Green)[4] when it is reflective rather than simply automatic or expected.

Reflectivity is an approach that welcomes 'blessing' because the final form has never quite emerged, and thus there is a need for encouragement and re-assurance on the way, in the procession. This is true of social reality as much as of personal awareness. Thus there is an profound place for the sacramental as the most important expression of truth as power, bringing together an element of material reality, and a capacity for further insight or effect, flexible with regard to both context and future possibilities.

For Charles Gore sacraments are the 'ceremonies of a society'[5], embodying principles within everyday life in a manner that invited deeper reflection and engagement beyond what might pass as 'knowledge' at that time. In this way sacraments nourish character, a proper expression of duty, and the possibilities for public opinion.

The church itself can be seen as a sacrament of the universal saving love of God expressed in moments of invitation in different times and cultures. This is a very different understanding of an exercise of power and its framing by 'Truth', than one based upon set texts, fixed practices and certain knowledge. This is why liturgy is central to the life of the church, as the laboratory inviting reflection, humility about being 'wrong' and openness to receiving new life.[6] Sacrament in particular practices, roles and resources that can affirm the desire to 'be ye perfect, even as Your Father ....' (Matthew 5[48]), not as an objective, quantifiable achievement, but in the way that a child can learn to move towards the fuller life of the parent.

Yet this path, or way, is never simply progressive or predictable. The 'wrongness' of much human endeavour requires not just illumination but redemption. The sheer unmerited triple gift of love through becoming embraced into the life of Father, Son and Holy Spirit.

This gift enables recognition not of miraculous events, but of expressions of the inner significance of human endeavour when humbly aligned with this particular kind of self-sacrificing openness to something as yet not fully known or experienced. Thus, Christian doctrine is not to be thought of as truth to be applied as a self-evident power – but rather to be appreciated as 'an expression of principles already implied in the ordinary procedure of reason, and partially embodied in the civilisation it was involved in creating'.[7]

Sacramentality is inherent in the processes of creation. Christian sacraments are specific models of this truth, endowed with a particular power to give focus and expression to what is true of the basic workings of creation. This is expressed in Romans 8 by St Paul's image of the whole creation struggling in labour pains (Roman 8^{22}) so that nothing can separate us from this love of God being ever offered into our lives.

Thus religion requires engagement with the world, rather than withdrawal from it – not to foster uncritical acceptance of what 'is', but for the church to witness through an ordering sacramentality to the truth of Mt. 8^{35}: 'those who want to save their life will lose it, and those who lose their life for my sake, and for the sake of the Gospel, will save it'. For those who live according to this truth of self-sacrifice the result is to be enabled to 'not taste death until they see that the Kingdom of God has come with power'.

The present is not abandoned for the future. Rather the present contains the necessary seeds of the future – seeds to be searched out and nourished appropriately to enable the growth of things which in appearance will emerge to be totally different, as in Hegel's image of the bud and the blossom.[8] Similarly, therefore, the church can never seek to form a distinctively 'ecclesiastical' life: her way of witness will be always though the groaning labour pains of the whole of creation. Because of the organic nature of reality, the self can only be realised in the realisation of society, by the way of self-sacrifice – which creates a powerful obligation or duty to participate in the common good, or in more biblical terms to participate in the procession of the Messiah towards the Heavenly City (John 12^{12-19}).

Thus, power is not rule over life, which has become a modern secular heresy. Rather, power is the energy which emerges from the triple gift of love to manifest the truth about creation, creatures and the call towards fulfilment: the way of salvation. This kind of power, and the resulting truth which emerges, is not therefore the result of cogito – human thinking as mastery and control. Rather it is the outcome of credo, a commitment of the 'wrong' which defines the self, into a sacrifice that opens up space for greater illumination. This is well expressed by Tina Beattie in her study of Thomas Aquinas and Jacques Lacan: "knowing truthfully is contemplative, to such an extent that the more thankfully we know, the more conscious we become of the mystery of which we are a part".[9]

The approach is best accessed through silence and the acceptance of fundamental secrecy: the path of prayer properly understood.

This explains why the missionary movement that unfolded through the leadership of St Paul was based upon testimony to the indwelling of Christ, rather than focussed in the systematic exposition of binding formulas or policies. The key foundation was the experience of presence – an openness to continuing encounter experienced as annunciation. We can see the whole of the missionary ministry of Jesus as a similar procession within which people and groups could taste something of the saving love of God, but generally within their own context, and not readily shaped to fit the existing patterns of religious belief or behaviour. The spirit brought disturbance and fraction as expressions of thanksgiving for

God's generous love. An aliveness to new and as yet unknown possibilities.

The key focus remained with the moments of annunciation – which become sacramental signs for further reflection. The stuff of prayer. Thus St Paul is clear that we are saved through faith: to believe is to be. Any 'knowledge' will be always emerging from this experience, and therefore a continuing and developing expression of faith: I believe (credo) therefore I am. While Greeks were seen by St Paul to elevate knowledge to something more controlling and determinative, just as Jews used tradition for similar purposes, in fact Christ crucified is "the power of God and the wisdom of God" (Corinthians 1[24]) for those who are 'called'. This emphasises the primacy of annunciation, calling out faith or a credo.

This makes clear that Christianity is not a form of knowledge but a way of life which makes knowing possible within particular contexts. Such different experiences of 'knowing' are held in a deeper faith – a common credo or dwelling in Christ. This was the basis of Paul's appeal to the competing parties in Corinth (I Corinthians 1), as much as it was for Samuel Wilberforce striving to be bishop of a whole diocese rather than to some of its 'parties'. Such faith is fed by a love that Christ wells up in each believer, as the power that nourishes, connects to others, and brings the embrace of the Heavenly Kingdom.

As Kierkegaard recognised,[10] such a God is essentially hidden, secret and within – and only made manifest indirectly – hence the significance of annunciation. The challenge is to explore the range of possible interpretations: the contrasting stories of Zechariah and Mary offer instructive models.

The result is that the Christian is always in the process of formation and more likely to be influenced by personal example and experience than systems or more formal scheme.

Annunciation offers the experience of 'presence' – in relation to oneself, one's situation and the power of the Creator. For Paul such presence was marked by an excess – of light, love, possibility. He needed the mediation of the others to interpret and manage this gift so that his initial credo could become an energy and an insight offering a ministry of similar mediation to others. Church members and structures have a key role in drawing out the gift and enabling its fuller expression, as the contribution of Ananias (Acts 9[10-19]) and the 'pillars' of the nascent church (Acts 21[18]) made clear in the case of Paul himself. Such ministries of mediation helped the power of love to move through the receiving response of 'I believe' into necessary action to reach out with such an excess of light and love to others.

The ultimate expression of this excess or grace, was the sense of being embraced into the Resurrection as the continuing and ever enduring means of annunciation.

Endnotes

[1] G. Watson, The English Ideology, Allen Lane 1973, p61.

[2] Ibid, p76.

[3] G. Watson, Ibid, p67.

[4] Ibid, p90.

[5] R. Kenyon, Theology, Vol 26, 1933: The Lux Mundi School, p20.

[6] Alastair Redfern, The Church: A Workshop of Salvation, ISPCK 2016.

[7] C.J. Webb, Religious Thought in England from 1850, Oxford 1933, p102.

[8] J. Stewart, Idealism and Existentialism, Continuum 2010, p21.

[9] Tina Beattie, Theology After Postmodernity, Oxford 2017, p37.

[10] J. Brejdak, The Thorn in The Flesh, LIT 2017, p41.

Epilogue

In our globalised and populist world where claims of 'fake news' and 'post-faith' jostle with scientific and sociological 'certainties' in terms of discerning, describing and developing what is claimed to be demonstrably 'true', the church as agent of the Gospel of Jesus Christ faces a number of considerable challenges.

Religion is no longer an identifiably geographic or cultural phenomenon. Rather it must take its place within a marketplace of values and viewpoints, all competing for attention and popular 'verification'. The last one hundred years have seen the growth of an assumed connectivity between the view of the majority and the definition of what must be right. Truth in this popular understanding is the contemporary expression of our understanding of sovereignty: the source and manifestation of the only power that should be recognised as legitimate.

In this scenario the gospel would take its place as one offer amongst many in a crowded and competitive market. The result tends to be a mirroring of successful business models, with an initial concentration upon securing a strong base through effective internal management to ensure a robust and reliable 'offer' or product.

The next stage is to develop a salesforce to compete and connect with potential consumers. Marks of success are rooted in strategy and expressed through sales. 'Truth' is packaged, promoted and consumed.

By contrast, as the argument of this book has tried to demonstrate – for Jesus, as for Paul, the foundation for values was neither geographical (not only in Jerusalem) nor ideological (challenging the Sabbath laws). Rather, the foundation for pursuing truth for individuals and communities was encounter or annunciation. On the way, in the procession which is the unfolding of human life in any of its manifestations. This is the stuff of what a modern prophet, Jacques Derrida, calls the necessary task of 'living together'.[1]

The way of this witness of encounter, seeking to participate in the gifting offered through annunciation, arises at an interesting moment in contemporary society. With a move towards smaller and less expensive Government, there is more space for social encounter, not least in civil society and through the necessary provision of welfare. The story of the entrepreneurial development of voluntary societies in the eighteenth century provides a creative model of the capacity of the people of faith to bring self-sacrificial service into places formerly occupied by carefully audited central and local government agencies. Systems giving way to faith based sacrificial service, the energy and creativity of willing volunteers able to adapt to micro contexts and shifts in need.

Further the opportunity for partnerships across different areas can re-establish wider awareness of civic and family type connectivity. This can provide another illustration of faith being a question pursued through the processions of life and a series of moving encounters – able to deliver not just care and support, but friendship, enlightenment and a genuine confidence in new life. Truth no longer envisaged as rights (no matter how popular to democratic majorities) but rather truth as an emerging awareness of richer possibilities in and between people. Truth emerging as annunciation enables and encourages: sustenance for a journey into resurrection.

This possibility may well chime with the shifting and plural context made so public through the development of social media – which provides a place for people not to play by the rules of traditional expectations, whether political, social or religious. Instead people pursue meaning in a world of hyper energy, reduced in extreme cases to emojis!, and content to operate in relativity limited spaces. This context can help Christian faith move from being perceived as rule based, to becoming a creative force for the flow of goodness – wherever it can be enabled and encouraged.

Just as Jesus enabled annunciation through meaningful encounter, so the current operation of the Gospel is challenged to trust in a similar approach to the pursuit of 'truth' which lies in every human heart.

In fact a major element in much of what might be characterised as contemporary civilisation is trust in reality perceived through 'therapy'. The strong belief in the possibilities of development and recovery, through reflection and increased self-awareness. Along with the growth of a 'therapeutic culture', which is often presumed for major humanitarian disasters as much as for individual needs, is a recognition of the importance of so much that seems to be beneath the surface of everyday living – desire, esteem, guilt, anxiety, freedom, theories of sexual motivation.

To reclaim the New Testament message that the truth indwells, and is properly nurtured through the inner life, has enormous potential for helping the struggles of our therapeutic culture to find more productive grounding in a faith commitment to the reconciliation and redemption of these elements into the more perfect fullness which they crave – a kingdom of eternal wholeness and perfection. Another instance of truth being met in questions and pursued on the journey of going both wider and deeper.

The procession towards truth is to be encountered through the questions arising from paying attention to annunciation in the everydayness of living. The church holds sacraments and scriptures to shape and inspire our capacity for noticing and responding, but only the dynamic between the person in their context and the institution guarding privileged resources, will enable any kind of shift from the wisdom of that initial silence modelled by Jesus before Pilate, to the journey through mortality into eternity. The Way, the Truth, the Life.

Endnotes

[1] H. de Vries & L.E. Sullivan, Political Theologies, Fordham University Press 2006, p3.

www.ingramcontent.com/pod-product-compliance
Lightning Source LLC
Chambersburg PA
CBHW051929240626
47153CB00004B/1426